"This is not a good book, or even a great book, but rather is an excellent book. The writers here have managed the near impossible by presenting stories that are not just touching, amusing, amazing, evocative, or poignant but also powerfully erotic. I cannot recommend it too highly!"

—M. Christian, author of *Dirty Words* and *The Bachelor Machine*

"Susie Bright and her amazing cadre of authors take you around the world emotionally as much as they do sexually."

—Carol Queen, Ph.D., Center for Sex and Culture, San Francisco, and author of *The Leather Daddy and the Femme* and *Real Live Nude Girl*

"Sex is messy, enchanting, perverse, and wondrous—so is this collection. I dare you not to cringe in places, and I double dare you not to be aroused."

—Phil "Satyrblade" Brucato, contributor, *NewWitch* magazine

"In *Three Kinds of Asking For It,* Susie Bright captures us in a trio of wickedly witty, tightly woven webs of erotic request. When released, the reader is sure to ask for more."

—Kathleen E. Morris author of *Speaking in Whispers: Lesbian African-American Erotica* and founder of The Erotic Pen Writing Workshops

"Be careful what you wish for! In these stories, the monkey's paw definitely gets its fingers burned. There's food here for your mind and your body, literary and pornographic. I know I'll find myself thinking much more about these stories as soon as I get through buzzing off. Good reading and guaranteed intelligent fun."

—Dossie Easton, coauthor of *The Ethical Slut* and *Radical Ecstasy*

"Everything you wished for and more; a delightful menage à trois. Albert, Christina, and Soloway position themselves in the forefront of contemporary erotica—and every other which way as well. Hot and licking good fun!"

—Lawrence Paros, author of *Bawdy Language*

OTHER BOOKS BY SUSIE BRIGHT

Three the Hard Way, editor

Mommy's Little Girl:
Susie Bright on Sex, Motherhood, Porn, and Cherry Pie

Best American Erotica 1993–2005, editor

How to Write a Dirty Story

Full Exposure

Nothing But the Girl (with Jill Posener)

The Sexual State of the Union

Sexwise

Susie Bright's Sexual Reality

Susie Sexpert's Lesbian Sex World

Herotica I, II, and III, editor

SUSIE BRIGHT

Presents

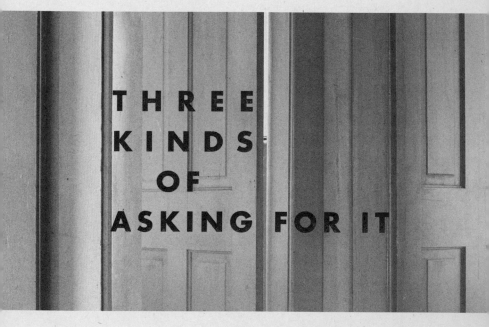

THREE KINDS OF ASKING FOR IT

EROTIC NOVELLAS BY

Eric Albert,

Greta Christina, and

Jill Soloway

A Touchstone Book
Published by Simon & Schuster
New York   London   Toronto   Sydney

TOUCHSTONE
Rockefeller Center
1230 Avenue of the Americas
New York, NY 10020

Introduction copyright © 2005 by Susie Bright
Charmed, I'm Sure copyright © 2005 by Eric Albert
Bending copyright © 2005 by Greta Christina
Jodi K copyright © 2005 by Jill Soloway

For information regarding special discounts for bulk purchases,
please contact Simon & Schuster Special Sales at 1-800-456-6798
or business@simonandschuster.com

Designed by Elliott Beard

Manufactured in the United States of America

10 9 8 7 6 5 4 3 2 1

Library of Congress Cataloging-in-Publication Data
Susie Bright presents : three kinds of asking for it : erotic novellas /
    by Eric Albert, Greta Christina, Jill Soloway.
        p. cm.
    "A Touchstone book."
    Contents: Charmed, I'm sure / Eric Albert—Bending / Greta Christina—
Jodi K / Jill Soloway.
    1. Erotic Stories, American. I. Title: Three kinds of asking for it.
II. Bright, Susie. III. Albert, Eric. Charmed, I'm sure. IV. Christina, Greta.
Bending. V. Soloway, Jill. Jodi K.
PS648.E7S868 2005   823'.01083'082—dc22   2004063397

ISBN-13: 978-0-7432-4550-0
ISBN-10:   0-7432-4550-4

CONTENTS

INTRODUCTION

There are certain lessons that are the catnip of erotic literature. "Be careful what you wish for" is a perfect example. It's an axiom that must have originated in lust. There's no other crazy yearning besides sex that makes people *so sure* that if they could possess just one thing, their ideal, then their bodies would know true bliss and their minds, a final epiphany. We imagine, with each new obsession, that our appetite will be sated for all time, and that our itch will melt into a sticky puddle. Free at last, and spent to peaceful exhaustion.

What's funny about human beings is that in our search for the perfect sex thing, the partner/position/pornography of our dreams, we never stay in one place. There's nary a moment for reflection before we switch targets. We laugh at teenagers who carry on as if one kiss, then one date, then one debauched prom night would make everything copacetic. But really, adults are worse. We blow our fortunes, our families' patience, and our own fatuous minds with schemes to become the perfect object of desire—or to capture one who is.

Sexual ecstasy is the prize that incites this madness. Once we conceive of our dream, and sample the first taste, we make the nuttiest promises. That's where the "be careful" part comes in. We vow, we forsake this and that, we say "nothing else matters." We jump off the deck and act as if pulling the cord is just an option. Who's around to see us when we land? Often, we end up on the ground alone, bruised and bloody, still carrying that taste in our mouth . . . *if only, if only, if only.* It's salty, all right.

Thank Cupid for novelists, then, who can admit the painful truth we might not confess to our own diaries. A good storyteller will describe a sexual adventure that makes us crave passion and cower before its consequences—in equal diabolical measures. It's difficult to find that chemistry in a novel. So many writers go overboard in one direction or another.

In puritan America, there's a tendency to choke the life out of those who have too much fun—unless of course, they get down on their knees and apologize for it later. The more rare, but equally cynical, experience is the story of the lovers who get everything they want, wrapped in a bow, and then sail off with their gift, undisturbed by the slightest breeze of conflict. They must be made of Spam.

Luckily, I've found three writers for this collection who bring uncommon originality and authenticity into the sweet mire of erotic trepidation.

In *Charmed, I'm Sure* by Eric Albert, a single man exasperated with conventional dating rituals meets a modern-day witch who sells him a sex-on-demand "Wish Contract." It seems to be the answer to his libidinous prayers, but then we all know how that fine print can screw you. . . . Our hero is in for more than any megawatt attorney could have anticipated.

Albert's work is the fount of carnal knowledge. He knows exactly how badly behaved people will act in order to get their rocks off, and furthermore, he'll have you on his side to urge them on. There will be no easy reckoning or soft landings, but he'll have his reader gnawing on the same bone by the time he's done.

In *Bending,* by Greta Christina, we have the story of a girl who can't get enough of one particular thing. It's bending over—literally. She's sick of having to say, "Okay, I'm through," when in fact she's never come close to her limit. Unlike most women, she's not prepared to fake and be demure. Her lovers and friends finally devise a scheme to test her endurance, and therein lies the tale.

The story seems so simple—a girl fixated on coming in her favorite position. (Show of hands, please?) But our heroine's walkabout to understand her desire and her unusual relationship with her lovers are eye-opening in their design. Her romance is with a greater community than two, and her vision is even bigger than her ass-up appetite.

Finally, in *Jodi K,* by Jill Soloway, we are introduced to a teenage diary, penned by a dentist's daughter in suburban Chicago. Jodi, our narrator, is savvy enough to realize that grown-ups are fixated on protecting and simultaneously exploiting her every sexual feeling for the "dirty parts"—but she's not about to leave any predictable droppings behind her.

Soloway has an uncanny ability to get *waaaay* inside the defiance, self-absorption, and havoc of the horny teenager's imagination. She makes it all seem as close as wet laundry—more than a little sweaty, and impossible to wriggle out of.

Introduction

These three authors didn't let their hell-and-lust-bent characters get off with anything the easy way. Their bed-tossed struggle was my delight; my vicarious thrills were pushed to their limits. I'm pleased to say I was still left gasping, "Oh yes, I'd do it all over again!" Isn't that what we always long to say— our parachute billowing around us, barely on the ground, the silk swirling at our feet?

Susie Bright
June 2005

CHARMED, I'M SURE

Eric Albert

For Oboe
Faithful companion
1984–2002

ACKNOWLEDGMENTS

I would like to acknowledge the following people for emotional and intellectual support; story ideas and structure; discussions; test reading; critical comments and suggestions; line editing; and copyediting. Thank you, thank you, thank you!

Prassede Calabi	Anonymous
Uncanny	Sia Stewart
Bárbara Selfridge	Deborah A. Levinson
Henry Gonshak	Alf
jude	Foggy Brume
Rain Man	Todd Belton
Jonathan A. Penyack	Valerie White
Anonymous	Anonymous

I also would like to acknowledge the wonderful *Roget's International Thesaurus, Fourth Edition,* the excellent *Webster's New World Dictionary, Third College Edition,* and the pretty darn good Microsoft Word 2000.

"So I can screw anyone I like?"

"You don't have to like them."

"Ah. Like, uh . . . like that black woman with the braids?" David pointed across the crowded hotel ballroom.

"Sure, if you get off on fake tits."

"They're fake?"

"You can have whoever you want. However you want. Whenever you want."

David's grin broadened. "OK, I'm impressed. That is one of the all-time great pickup lines. Now, what do you really do?"

"Exactly what I said. Look, here's my card."

"Mm. Melissa Natrova, Witch. Spells, charms, sundry magick . . . witches have web sites?"

"Fax machines, too. Does my offer interest you?"

David examined her. She was petite and pretty. No, not pretty—something deeper and better. Her unlined face was bordered with copper-red hair that brought out the fire in her amber eyes. "You don't look like a witch."

"When I come to these things as a 112-year-old hag, I don't get hit on nearly so much."

David blinked. He would have taken her for thirty, tops. Her butt didn't look a day over twenty-eight.

"Why *does* a witch come to a singles night?"

She shrugged. "Same reason lawyers gather at a train wreck. I probably do two-thirds of my business at events like this."

"People actually pay for your help?"

"People pay for *this*." She swung her arm to indicate the awkward attendees, the faux-hip faux-hip-hop graffiti banners, the busy cash bar. She looked at him. "You, for instance. Surely there's some more entertaining way you could be spending this evening."

"Like sitting at home obsessing about my ex?"

"Divorced, huh?"

"No. Betrayed." David's grin was now more a grimace.

"Oh?"

"Yeah. We lived together for six years. Up and down, very volatile, high highs and vicious lows. We had some unbelievable times. Then Iris left me for another guy."

She looked him over. "You're, what, thirty-five?"

"Thirty-six."

She nodded. "In your prime earning years. And you're not ugly—cute even, if you'd do something hipper with your hair. You make eye contact, you checked my ass without being a jerk, you meet minimum conversational standards. Why'd she walk?"

"She felt I had a temper problem."

"Do you?"

"Maybe." He paused. "But I was working on it. She should have stayed."

"She didn't. And now you're here."

"It's been seven months. Time to ride the horse that threw me."

She smiled, showing impeccable teeth. "'Get back in the saddle' is more like it, Dave. You're not ready for a new relationship. You're looking to get laid."

David searched a moment for words. "I've lost my trust in women. Or maybe just misplaced it. But till I get it back, what's wrong with pleasure?"

"Nothing's wrong with pleasure. What's wrong is wasting hours here, hoping to find someone drunk or desperate enough to take you home. Why not use my services? You can skip the deep discussions—just tell 'em to bend over. And forget about these leftovers." She waved her hand dismissively at the crowd. "You can have anyone: your neighbor, your neighbor's daughter, your boss. Your wish is their command."

"My boss is a man."

"Sex is sex."

"Let me rephrase that. My boss is a bipolar egomaniac who reads *Dilbert* for management tips."

"Fine. But do you take my point?"

David couldn't hold back a sheepish smile. "Yeah, I take your point. But how do I know you're a witch?"

"The business card didn't do it? I had those suckers printed in four colors."

He looked at her.

"OK, OK. One free spell coming up."

She closed her eyes. Something fled her face and, for an instant, he could see a century in her skin. She took three slow, deep breaths. She murmured half a dozen words that weren't anything like English.

"Oh." David stiffened, then stood statue still, the warmth of the sensation surging, spreading.

"Sweet, hey? Imagine if that was a real tongue."

A minute drifted past. The witch spoke three short words and opened her eyes.

"So, David. Would you like to sign up?"

A shudder slipped through David's body. He rubbed the back of his neck gently. His eyes met hers.

"What's the price?" he said warily. "My soul?"

"There's six billion people in the world nowadays. A soul goes for thirty-five bucks, give or take—one of those supply-demand things. I work for real money."

"What's real money?"

"The standard one-day all-you-can-eat package is yours for just four thousand."

"Dollars?"

He sensed heads turning. The witch nodded cheerfully.

"Do the math. A good call girl will run you three hundred an hour in this city. That's twenty-four hundred a day, for one person in one room. I offer you everyone in the world, everywhere in the world. Plus exceptional customer support."

"I don't use prostitutes."

"And I don't employ them. I deal in sex slaves."

He winced. "Nice language."

"But I *mean* slaves, David. They'll do anything you say, things you couldn't pay a street whore to do. *Anything.*" The witch leaned forward. Her voice dropped to a whisper. "*Fuck* trust—you'll have total control."

He felt like he'd been punched, softly, inside his stomach.

His body believed her.

And so did he.

"I don't have anything like four thousand in cash."

She grinned and straightened up, suddenly more businesslike. "Who does? I take credit cards, EFTs, checks written on major in-city banks, and stock held in your name. Oh, and bullion."

"Visa OK?"

"Absolutely. Anything but American Express and their 'we do not service adult-oriented businesses' policy." She singsonged the words. "Give me a damn break."

"Do we do this now, or what?"

"Now's always my favorite time. Let's get some privacy."

He followed her through the double doors into the lobby. She went to the coat-check counter and handed a ticket to a young woman with five rings in her ear, receiving in return a brown leather portfolio. David and the witch moved to a pair of armchairs by a circular glass table holding a shaded lamp. The witch opened the portfolio and slid out some papers.

"Here's a contract. It covers the details of what we've been chatting about."

David laid the pages on the table and started to read. Several clauses later, he looked up. "Shouldn't I know how the magic works before I commit to anything?"

"If you understood it, it wouldn't be magic. Anyway, magic has a mind of its own—you never know just what it'll do. This magic makes others extremely susceptible to your sexual commands. What's sex and what's not sex isn't always clear, but if the magic's feeling friendly, you'll get a lot of leeway. Still, I wouldn't recommend telling people to give you money or inside information. If it turns on you, magic can get mighty mean."

"I'll watch myself. But I meant, what do I do to put a spell on someone?"

"Oh, that's a different question. Ready? Make fists, then stick out your index fingers. Put your left index finger between your lips, touching your teeth. And put your right index finger in your ear. Perfect."

"I have to do this every time I want sex?" he mumbled.

"Oh, no. You do this when you want to amuse me. For sex, you need a talisman."

David slowly lowered his hands. "Does your smartass attitude ever cost you customers?"

"Not so's I've noticed. The service basically sells itself— men'll do anything to avoid foreplay."

She searched through her portfolio. "Ah, here we go." She produced a small cloth bag, blue as an August sky. It glittered in the incandescent light. She loosened the drawstring, reached inside, and brought out a green sphere a little larger than a marble. She placed it on his palm.

He saw that the charm's surface was rough, pocked, cratered like the moon. He turned it slowly in his fingers.

"Keep that close by. When the mood strikes, hold it and say *avrat taldor.* Whoever hears will mind your words."

"*Avrat taldor?*"

"Close enough for magic. If you forget the phrase, just remember it's *rodlat tarva* backward."

David pushed the charm into his pocket and went back to

the contract. He read slowly, keeping place with the edge of his hand. When he was done, he returned to the start.

"This clause says I can control both women and men. Suppose I don't want sex with a guy."

"Then don't stick your dick in one. It's unlikely to happen by accident."

". . . Right." He turned to the next page. "And here it says the charm works from nine A.M. to five P.M. You said a day."

"Nine to five *is* a standard business day."

"For four thousand, I want twenty-four hours."

"And I want to be ninety again. I'll hold my breath if you will . . . or we could compromise on nine to nine."

"I like sex late. Make it nine to midnight."

"You understand, I'm the one who answers the phone. That would be one long day. For both of us."

"I'll hold my breath if you will."

The corners of the witch's mouth twitched. "Right." She took the contract, marked the change, and initialed it. "Anything else?"

"Yeah. Diseases."

"Two fifty gets you the STD Rider, which keeps you, and anyone involved with you, safe from bugs. No pus, no fuss. The rider also includes PPP—Pregnancy Protection for Partners." She handed him another page.

He read it carefully. "Looks OK."

"Good. Fill in your personal information here and here, and sign here. Give me your card and I'll run it while you finish off."

"Do I need to sign in blood?"

"No, it photocopies poorly. Here's a pen."

* * *

The alarm woke David from his dream of coaching a women's synchronized skinny-dipping team. He showered slowly and dressed quickly. A banana and a sticky bun were breakfast as he read the center columns of the *Wall Street Journal*.

He looked into his bedroom. Sprawled on the bed's comforter, in the sun-soaked spot by the window, lay his cat, the morning's light bringing out the brown fur beneath his black tipping.

"Oboe."

The cat's ears sharpened and his tail thumped once. David got on the bed and laid his cheek on the cat's side. Through the warmth, the thrumming was so low that he felt rather than heard it.

"Do you believe in witches, Oboe? 'Cause I don't." Oboe purred. "Which means I've let some crazy woman put four big ones on my credit card. I should refuse the charge." Oboe stretched slowly and fully until the tips of his paws vibrated. "Except I signed that contract. Shit. What'll I do?" Oboe purred. "Go to work, I guess. You have a good day now—don't overstress."

David left his apartment and entered June: sunny, a little cool, the rosebush hedge plastered with small red blooms. He hated to close the car door on it. He drove into the city, parked under his building, and took the elevator fifteen floors. He chatted for a moment with the receptionist, then walked down the hall to his office with its wall of windows overlooking the city.

He began working his way through the morning's e-mail. Unthinkingly, he took out the green ball and massaged its cool, rough surface. He envied Catholics their beads: how nice to prepare yourself for everlasting life by making little motions with your hands.

There was a knock on the door.

"Come in."

A woman walked in, closing the door behind her. David swiveled his chair and eyed her warily.

"Janet. How's it going?"

"OK. Could be better. You could make it better."

"The Morgan thing again?"

"Again? You haven't given me anything yet." Janet's eyes were ice.

"I got you a draft two weeks ago."

"Nothing *useful* yet. The client wants this done last Monday."

David's voice softened. "Screw Morgan and his asinine deadlines. Chandler is all over me to ride herd on the TIMS project."

"That's your problem. Chandler's not my boss."

"And Morgan's not my client, Janet. Have someone in your own damn group do it."

"You know we don't have anyone with your skills. And this has to be done right. Morgan's a nitpicky bastard. If he cuts the cord now, it's my ass."

Anger shimmered between them like heat waves on a highway. David's hands made fists. The charm was warm against his palm. Why not. Why the hell not.

"*Avrat taldor.*"

"What?"

"Show me that ass."

Janet turned away. He waited for her to stalk out in rage. It wouldn't be the first time.

Janet stayed.

Three seconds passed before understanding flooded David. With it came a feral glee that set his pulse dancing. This was magic, strong magic. He opened his hand and smiled at the charm. It glowed softly. He dropped it into his breast pocket. He looked over at Janet.

"David, what's—"

"Lift your skirt to your waist. Slowly."

Janet grasped the fabric near her hips and gathered it into her hands. The hem of her skirt rose like a curtain. David watched as wonders were revealed. Calves. Thighs. Sky blue cotton.

"What the hell's going on?"

"You're showing me your panties."

"What the . . . what is . . . why are we doing this?"

"I'm doing it because I can. You're doing it because I told you to. Bend over."

Janet bent. David could see the muscles in her arms as she gripped her bunched skirt tight. Her panties swelled. He thrilled with his new-bought power, gazing hungrily at the submitting woman. "I can't believe you're doing this."

"*Stop it.* I don't want this."

"But how can you resist? I'm such a charming guy."

"Fuck you."

"Oh, we'll get to that, Janet. We will definitely get to that. You know, you've got a good-looking ass."

"Let me go. Now."

"Take off your panties. Now."

She let go of her skirt and pulled her panties down with a jerk. David caught a flash of flesh before the curtain fell. Janet awkwardly shuffled her feet and the panties appeared at her ankles. She stepped out of them, leaving a mound of blue on the floor.

"Give them to me."

Janet turned to pick up the panties, then stood. She crumpled the garment and hurled it as hard as she could. The panties blossomed in midair. David lazily caught them and dropped them on his lap. His hard lap.

Aggressive, alert, completely focused—he felt perfect. He was in the moment, not near it, or alongside it, but smack fuck *in* it. Anger had always been his drug of choice, and he was back in the maw of the monster.

"Good girl."

"Say that again and I'll break every bone in your face." Her words were undercut by the confusion in her eyes.

"Unbutton your blouse."

She stared ahead as her hands worked the buttons.

"Take it off . . . good. Drop it on the floor. Mmm, you really fill out that bra. I'd like to see what's underneath."

Silence.

"That wasn't a rhetorical observation, Janet. Give me your bra."

Janet turned her bare back to him. She slipped the straps off her shoulders and pulled the bra around to undo the clasp. She tossed the bra backward toward his voice, then stood stiff and straight in her skirt and shoes.

"Don't you want to show 'em to me?"

The tension in her shoulders was her response.

"Still playing hard to get. OK, go to the windows." David swiveled to keep her in view. "Now hold your arms up and press your tits against the glass. Harder, really flatten 'em. Yes. There, you're safe from my eyes. Feel better?"

"Stop it, stop it, *stop it.*"

"Would you rather let me see?"

"I don't want *anyone* to see."

"Bullshit. You've had half the men on this floor. I can't grab a cup of coffee without hearing from some new guy in your menagerie."

"Who I do is my business."

"Not anymore, Janet."

David retrieved her bra from the floor and placed it on his desk along with her panties. He moved to just behind her and looked over her shoulder at the forest of office buildings.

"I love this view. And all those people have a great view, too. Imagine how you look."

There was a knock on the door, and Janet let out a whimper.

"Huh. Another guy who wants to see your tits. 'Course, he probably has already. Why don't you go see who it is."

Janet, arms high, breasts squashed against the pane, shook her head violently.

"You know I can make you do it."

Janet pressed her forehead against the glass and gave the tiniest of nods.

His mouth was an inch from her ear, whispering. "Looks like I can make you do anything I want. Run your afternoon meeting bare-assed. Send dirty e-mail to Morgan. Crawl on hands and knees through the corridors, begging for cocks to suck. Except you already do that, you fucking slut. Am I the only guy who hasn't smeared your lipstick with his dick?"

"But you had a girlfriend."

"Not recently. And Alex was married. Why don't you ever—"

There was another knock.

"Let's ask them in." He headed for the door.

"David."

He ignored her.

"David!"

His hand was on the knob.

"I'm showing you, David. *Look,* damn it."

He opened the door a crack. "Casey, hey. Can it wait? I'm meeting with a client. . . . Sure, three work? Great."

The door clicked shut as he turned to face the topless Janet. "Good girl! Why were you so bashful? You've got great tits. And the window has done wonders for your nipples."

The skin across Janet's cheekbones was taut.

"Now, won't you shake those big breasts for me?"

Her eyes turned soft and glistened. "I'd rather suck donkey dicks in hell."

"Sweet, Janet. Put your hands behind your neck and shake 'em."

"You." Shake. *"Fucking."* Shake. "Ass." Shake. "Hole." Shake.

"Bouncing your boobs for me. Who'da thought it." He pointed to his crotch, where his pants were poking out. "It gets me right here. You horny, too?"

"No!"

"Tell the truth."

"No. Maybe. I don't know."

"What turns you on? What fills your fantasies?"

"The same stupid things excite everybody."

"Tell me."

Janet bowed her head. "Being restrained. And raped." Her voice was low.

"Isn't this your lucky day. What else."

". . . Multiple men. Teenage boys."

"What else."

She closed her eyes. "A big black dog."

"What do you do with the dog?"

"Fellatio. Then, then intercourse."

"You like it?"

"In my fantasy."

"What else."

"Being told what to do."

"Like this."

"In my fantasy."

"This is no fantasy."

Silence. She raised her head and looked at him. Her eyes and nipples were huge. He continued his catechism.

"What's the dirtiest thing you've done at work?"

". . . I was with James and Casey. Casey's office."

"Doing what?"

"Sucking. Back and forth between them."

"That excite you?"

"Yes."

"How can *I* excite you?"

"Oh god."

"Tell me. Tell me what to do."

"Oh god, oh god." She slapped her own cheek. "Oh god. Call me . . . call me *cunt.*"

"That's easy, cunt."

"Don't do this, David."

"What else, *cunt?* What else do you want from me?"

"Please."

"Tell me, you fucking cunt."

"Oh god. Fuck me. Don't ask, don't talk. Just take it."

"*Now* you want my cock? Two years you keep me high and dry, but I treat you like the slut you are and suddenly there's room between your legs."

A tear slid down her cheek. David's anger flickered for a moment. How much is too much? But his erection pulsed inside his pants.

"Lie across my desk." He pushed his papers and her underwear to the side. "Here." She lowered herself, breasts first, onto the desk. "More toward me." Now her breasts were hanging off the near edge, her legs projecting awkwardly off the back.

"Play with yourself. Come on, show me how you do it."

Janet licked the middle fingers of her right hand. She rolled a little onto her side to make space, moved her hands down to her crotch, then settled back on top of them. Her body jiggled slightly, the only hint of what she was doing.

"Yes. Get good and hot. But don't come."

He leaned over and twitched her skirt up onto her lower back, exposing her bare buttocks. He cupped the back of her head in his hands and rubbed his hard crotch against her lips, feeling her warm breath through the fabric of his pants.

"Yes. That's my good cunt. Work yourself."

He saw her buttocks clench and release, clench and release. He saw her brow furrow in concentration. Her breasts wobbled delicately. He took the nipples in his hands and tugged downward, stretching her nipples and breasts. He swung her breasts from side to side, using the nipples as handles. He squeezed until she yelped. She kept on masturbating.

He let go of her nipples and took a step back, then undid his belt and pushed his pants and underpants down a few inches. The head of his cock bobbed near Janet's lips. Her breaths were fast and shallow.

"You getting there?"

Janet nodded, her eyes half dull, half focused on his hard-on.

"Good. Don't you fucking come."

She moaned.

"Beg me to fuck you."

"Oh god. Please fuck me." Her forehead was misted with moisture.

He gripped his penis. "You can do better than that."

"*Please* fuck me. Put that in me. All the way in. Can I come now?"

"No. Beg."

"Fuck me. . . . Screw me. Ball me. . . . Bang me." Her eyes were leaking tears.

"More." He was stroking himself with one hand, cupping his balls with the other.

"I'm sopping wet inside. You'll love the way it feels. Please. Please. *Fuck me.*"

"I wouldn't piss on you if your twat was on fire. Now come, you fucking cunt."

Janet's body stiffened in orgasm, arching upward like a bow. Strange splutterings came from her mouth, and her eyes rolled halfway up in her head. David's penis erupted. He'd never come so hard. Or so much. His semen spat out in thick spurts, landing on the lingerie beside Janet's body, soaking it.

And still they both were coming. And coming.

David's penis stopped pumping at last, and he collapsed into his chair. His crumpled pants were lumpy underneath him. Janet subsided on the desk as her body thawed back to flesh. Her head hung down and her body was still.

After a minute, she clambered off the desk, swaying slightly, uneasy in her balance. Her hair was tangled and her cheeks were wet. She bent to get her blouse, her breasts swinging freely.

"Don't forget to put these on." David held up her soggy underwear. "And keep them on."

Janet took her panties from his hand, stepped into them, and pulled them up, making no attempt to screen the flash of pubic hair when she raised her skirt. She took her bra and mechanically refastened it. She put on her blouse. Semen from her bra instantly seeped through, forming dark blotches across her chest.

"Now get the fuck out of here. Cunt."

She left.

"Lonely Hearts Line, Grind House, and Chowder & Marching Society."

"It's David."

"Dave! Short time, no hear. Got your wick dipped and your dick whipped?"

"Stuff got all fucked up."

"Oh, no. Tell me where it hurts. Customer satisfaction is my middle name."

"The damn charm. I mean, she did everything I said . . ."

"Good."

". . . but she was fighting all the time."

"And . . ."

"I lost it. Things got ugly."

"And . . ."

"And nothing." His frustration boiled over. "The point is that I thought she'd . . . acquiesce."

The witch chuckled. "A peculiar thought."

"But . . ."

"But what? You can fuck anyone, anywhere. That's what I promised, that's what you got."

"Oh, come on . . ."

"You got off, right?"

"That's not the point." His voice rose in anger. "She was crying. Even when she was coming, she was crying. I don't want sex with me to be a punishment."

"*Chacun à son dégoût.* But anything for a client. Four hundred dollars gets you the Acceptance Rider."

"What the . . . what is that?"

"It makes others accept your authority without question or complaint."

"Will it make them happy?"

"Whoa. It takes the edge off interactions. It lowers the odds of someone calling the cops. You want to make a woman happy, buy her chocolate."

"Why the hell didn't you tell me about it before?"

"Why the hell did you sign a contract without due diligence?"

"Due diligence? Who would pay to spend a day browbeating miserable women into humiliating sex?"

"Just about every one of my clients."

*   *   *

David stood at the rear of his office and gazed at the city below, taking slow breaths to calm himself. He had the charm, he had the Acceptance Rider. There was plenty he could do, and only one day to do it in. *Let it go.*

He sent a message to his group and his boss, saying he'd be out the rest of the day on personal matters. Very personal matters, he thought.

He edged his car back up into the sunlight, feeling like he was playing hooky. Except, of course, he'd never skipped school, or anything else, in his life. The sudden freedom lifted his spirits, and he relaxed into the day and the songs on the radio. He let the car take him where it would.

When the commercial break came, he found himself on a tree-lined street in a western suburb that bordered his own. He parked in the dappled shade of a sidewalk maple and walked the brick path through the still day.

Iris answered the doorbell in a full-length maroon bathrobe.

"David. What are you doing here?"

"I wanted to talk."

"After all these months? I have nothing new to say. And I've got a piece due Monday."

"I want you back."

She shook her head slowly. "You have nothing new to say either."

"I'd like another chance."

"You had six years of chances in this house." Her voice was weary. "You know, I finally fixed the window that you cracked."

"I can make it up to you."

"*You bit my toe in the middle of the night.* You can't make that up."

". . . I'm sorry."

"I know you are. You always are. It's not enough."

She began to close the door.

"But I've been working hard. Medication, therapy. Thinking." David had his palms up, a ballplayer pleading for a call.

"Those are good things, and I'm glad you're doing them. But do them for yourself, not me. I'm taken."

That stung. "By Rob? Rob couldn't take you if you were bound spread-eagle with a ribbon around your neck."

"He doesn't make me cry."

"But does he fuck you till you scream?"

She paused. "What's it to you?"

"A lot. It meant a lot to you, too. Right?"

"Maybe." Her voice was wary.

He was flailing, failing. He jammed his hand into his pocket and found the charm. "*Avrat taldor.* Let me remind you. Let me in."

She looked troubled. After a long moment, she stepped aside. He pushed quickly past her into the house.

She followed him to the living room. The two of them stood silently. He looked around, rediscovering the old world. This was where they'd watched Celtics games. Where he'd read to her. Where she'd first offered sex to him. For months, he'd practiced words for now, but now they made no sense.

His eyes settled on her. "Take it off."

Her face went blank. Her hands fumbled for the sash, found it, undid it. She shrugged out of the robe, letting it fall to the floor like a shed skin. Naked, she looked awkward: right breast noticeably smaller, thick thighs, no hips. Her body had never done much for him—it was what she'd let him do to it.

"On your knees." He cracked the command like a whip.

She lowered herself to the blue Oriental rug, slipping soundlessly into their well-worn ritual.

"Take it out."

She unzipped his fly and tugged his pants and underpants down.

"Balls."

She took in a long breath, then dipped her head. She methodically bathed his balls with her tongue, her nose deep in his crotch hair. She worked her way to the underside. This was Iris doing this. Iris. His penis lay across her cheek, lengthening as she licked.

"Cock."

She put her arms behind her back, right hand grasping left wrist. She tilted her head to the side and caught the tip of his half-erect penis with her lips, then straightened and smoothly took him in. Her mouth was warm and wet. She bobbed her head slowly, finding her way to his rhythm.

He looked down on the part that split her light brown hair. So hot to have her there before him, below him. "Still like eating dick?"

She mumbled her assent.

"My dick?"

Another mumble.

"That's my little cocksucker. That's my good girl."

She sighed softly through her nose, and he felt a rush of triumph. He knew that sound: she was hooked, rapt, lost. His again.

He patted the back of her head once. She forced her face into his crotch, pushing the head of his penis into her throat's opening. He grunted. So smooth. He wondered if she kept in practice. He gripped her head and held her there. Her arms flexed behind her back, but she stayed still. He counted ten, then disengaged. She coughed and drew an arm across her eyes.

"Let's go upstairs," he said. He helped her up.

He followed her, his erection a compass and her naked buttocks north. She took him to her bedroom. He saw a bureau photograph of her and Rob in fluorescent ski outfits. Their bedroom.

"How's sex with Robbie?"

"Fine."

"Good as with me?"

"I don't compare."

David took her arm. "The hell you don't. Tell me what you miss."

She shook free and looked at him defiantly. "Doggy-style."

"He won't fuck you from behind?"

"He feels it would degrade me." Defiance masked defensiveness. She flinched when David laughed.

"As if. Get on the bed. Hands and knees. Head down, butt up."

Iris obeyed. David surveyed her. *The* position. Submissiveness incarnate. Some atavistic impulse made him ache to ravage all her holes at once, to fuck her senseless.

He got on the bed and knelt behind her. He put his penis at her opening. Half a year of fantasies come true. He rested his palms lightly on her back. "Miss me?"

The words hung in the air for seconds. "Sometimes."

He entered her. Slowly. Savoring each quarter inch of territory. Then back out. And in. And out. Quicker. He rocked his pelvis in the satisfying rhythm of the centuries.

"Squeeze," he said.

Iris tightened down, increasing friction all along his penis. So good.

"You're a well-trained slut."

A stronger squeeze.

"Who trained you?"

". . . You did." Shame mingled with excitement in her voice.

David moved inside her. He stiffened his penis and instantly she sighed with pleasure. Like old times. He stiffened his penis again and then again, loving the louder and louder moans he drew from her. He gripped her hips and took her faster. Her head swung wildly side to side. He hammered her home. She was yelling as she came. Her vaginal muscles went on automatic, hugging, slacking, hugging, slacking.

He'd done it. Relief washed over him. Now things would be easy. He slowed his thrusts to prime her, then rode her hard. In seconds, she was screaming out her lungs again. He pushed her to another potent orgasm. And another.

"That's my noisy girl. You need someone to put you through your paces."

He settled into a canter. He watched his penis gliding in and out of her. The sight was so familiar it was strange. He began the cycle yet again: slow, deep strokes to rev her up; fast, hard strokes to get her off. He suddenly stopped moving.

"No, don't," she gasped. "I'm almost there."

"I know. You do some work."

Iris rocked back, engulfing him. She rocked forward, stopping just before she lost him. She rocked back and forth, slowly, steadily, getting louder as she found her stride.

The phone on the bedside table rang. She halted midway on his penis. Another ring.

"Take the call, Iris."

She stretched carefully, keeping him inside, and reached for the phone. She rested on her elbows so she could hold it to her ear.

"Hello. Oh, hi, honey."

He'd known it would be Rob. His replacement. David wanted to claw, to scratch, to bite. But temperance, not temper. He leaned forward and murmured, "Fuck me, darling."

Iris started rocking again. She spoke into the phone. "Things are going well. I think I'll finish by tomorrow."

David stiffened his penis and Iris hissed. *Can't ignore me now, girl.*

"I'm leaning toward the pale yellow. It'll look darker once it's up."

Iris rocked slowly. He knew she was struggling to keep control. He needed her to lose that fight. He met her with a small thrust forward, so her buttocks banged his crotch. Again. Again. Again. His penis felt her tighten. She clamped her hand across her mouth. He gave her three strong, stiff strokes. Her body shook violently, and she dropped the phone. Her muscles spasmed around his penis. He came hard, spurting deep inside her. She collapsed on the bed, and he collapsed on her, chest to back. She was soaked with sweat.

She grabbed the phone. "Sorry, what was that, honey? . . . Oh, I plan to ask Lynn for her opinion first. We'll be living with this for years. I'll let you know what she says. . . . See you at six. Love you. Bye."

She lay beneath him, panting heavily, not moving. His penis slowly shrank, then slipped out. He peeled his skin from hers. They rolled onto their sides, face close to face. He looked into her hazel eyes.

"You liked that."

She nodded gently. "But what am I going to tell Rob?"

"About my come in your cunt? Lie to him. Like you did to me."

"I don't do that anymore."

Iris's words held quiet confidence. How unlike her. David frowned, then regrouped.

"Remember when I took you in that London phone booth?"

"With all the people from the station walking by."

"Yes."

She smiled. "I remember."

"And the time we visited your mom? That motel where I put my whole hand in you?"

"Mm-hm."

"You said you'd never come so hard."

"That's true. Then I said something wrong, like always, and you sulked. I wound up sleeping in the tub. I woke up when you drenched me with cold water." Her tone was matter-of-fact.

He had forgotten that. And maybe other things. Her calmness disconcerted him. He knew how to handle a raging, crazy Iris, but not this self-possessed woman. Something menaced him, lurking just outside his field of vision.

He shook it off. "Remember this?" He leapt up and dragged

her by her ankles down the bed, stopping when her buttocks reached the edge. He moved to the floor, sitting cross-legged at the foot of the bed, and guided her legs down and back so that her feet met between his thighs. He spread her knees, then leaned forward until they were snug around his shoulders.

He knew how it excited her to be "cunt front," exposed and accessible, her genitals the focus of her body. He loved her hairiness, the thick mat of golden-brown that spread out from her center, now darkened in the middle with her juice. He tenderly spread her, separating sticky strands to reveal her wrinkled treasure.

He bowed his head and closed his eyes and breathed. *There* it was. The scent he'd longed for. He did nothing but breathe, a shipwreck survivor who finds a spar to bear his weight. He nuzzled desperately, wetting his nose in her. Breath in, breath out. Inspiration, exultation.

He thumbed aside some errant hairs and put his mouth upon her. He heard a groan from far away. Her taste exploded in his mouth. Thick, sweet honey from her orgasms. The peppery savor of sweat. The buzzy numbing of his semen. He lapped.

Her clitoris was soft, asleep, and barely bulged beneath his tongue. No haste. He lapped. He pushed his tongue inside to gather extra honey.

He swept his tongue down to her other opening. He pressed apart her buttocks to get some breathing room. He touched her with his tongue's tip and tasted mustard. Her anal muscle spasmed and released. He tapped her with his tongue. Each contact brought another squeeze, a further letting go. He played her muscle's reflex, darting in on the release. Each venture took him further, until her clenching captured half his tongue.

He raised his head. Beyond the forest of her hair, he saw her breasts relaxing on her chest. He couldn't see her face. Who was it he was eating?

He placed his palms along her lips and spread them to make her clitoris pop up. He pressed his mouth against her taut skin, encircling the bud. Her lips nestled around his. His hands slipped down to rest upon his thighs. Her pubic hair brushed soft against his cheeks. His eyelids drifted shut. Home again.

He licked upward once. She sighed. He paused. He licked again. A suck. Another lick. A sigh.

Her clitoris was half awake. He swept the top with quick, light strokes. Then half a dozen smooth, sure laps, up and down, to make her groan and rouse her body.

He stopped, his mouth an O around her clit, shielding it from stimulation, and waited for her frustrated sigh. Then he went back to single strokes, now north-northwest, prodding the delicate underside at the spot that made her melt. He measured each stroke out, gasp by gasp, the strokes distinct, pickets of white pleasure standing sharp against a flat blue sky.

He dipped his tongue inside to get new juice, still copious, but no longer thick. The taste had mellowed, too.

Again he spread the skin beside her lips and brought his mouth to bear. He took in a long breath through his nose. He let it trickle out. He let the world fade. The Zen of cunnilingus.

He began to lick her gently with an easy rhythm. Her clitoris was full now, calling for attention, transmuting it to rapture, then transmitting it throughout her. He kept his licking steady to weave a haze of pleasure, diffuse and drifting, seeping through her body on the network of her nerves.

Muscles deep in foreign lands awoke. Her gasps had ceased.

Instead, her every breath was heavy, heightened, and, beneath, a murmuring, a blurring of some words. He didn't understand what she was saying; he doubted she did either. In any case, he didn't need a map—he knew the way, and now he led.

He also knew the kinds of images that filled her thoughts: she was the favor at a party, and a line had formed to take her; she was blindfolded, bound, with strangers pissing in her mouth; three men had plugged her holes so that all she knew was cock.

At times, he swirled his tongue in flourishes along her flesh, but always he returned to steady licking. He meant to be her rock, her refuge, the home where she was cared for. He licked, lost in her body, and she lay, lost in her head.

The licking brought him comfort. He might appear asleep, or deep in reverie, with nothing going on. But he was bathed in constant information from her clit and breath and muscles. He didn't need to think. He needed not to think.

He trailed his fingers lightly across her lower trunk in slow circles, edging down until he reached her honey fleece. He lifted his hands and brushed her hair ends, quickening the skin below. He moved on to her upper thighs, his touch still soft, spreading gooseflesh as he went. His hands glided down her inner thighs, meeting at the furrow of her buttocks. Her whole delta was astir.

Should he touch her anus? It would charge her, surge her, send a bolt of energy careening through her wires. A fingertip, circling slowly just inside her rectum, could make her come all on its own.

No. That seemed artificial, forced, impatient. He didn't want to flip a switch. He wanted her to float along, flowing with the current, a world of time, until she reached the falls.

And all the while, he licked. His licking took nothing out of him; it gave him peace. Lazy, seemingly undirected, touch after touch, like brushstrokes on a wall, each small, each meaningless, until you step back and find the wall is blinding white.

He opened his eyes, his mouth still fixed to her, his tongue still moving. Her breasts were covered with her gently kneading hands. Her hands rose, and she skated her palms across the tips of her nipples. *Of course.* So many nights he'd lain in bed, his hand around his penis, reliving every detail of their sex, and yet this thing she did had vanished from his memory. Obsession is a defense against loss, but there is no defense against loss.

He became aware of her knees squeezing his shoulders. Her soles no longer rested on the floor between his legs; her feet now arched, her toes pressed hard against the wood. Her clitoris was engorged, hard and round as a bead. He licked her strongly several times, his tongue rubbing up and down in firm, connected strokes. She moaned low and loud.

He loved this part, when everything he did felt fabulous to her. He reveled in his mastery, and knew no one else would ever eat her this well. She was in thrall to the smallest motion of his tongue. Her life—her house, her project, Rob—had disappeared. All she cared about was him.

He licked more lightly, not teasing her, still covering her clit each stroke, but letting her edge closer to orgasm. The challenge now was to keep her from slipping prematurely into weak bliss.

She pressed her crotch against his face, mashing his lips so hard they hurt. Brute force against the circle around her clitoris, but, inside, subtlety and nuance as his gentle licking continued. He slid his hands under her buttocks, feeling the flesh adjust to his palms. He gripped her with his fingers and heard her sharp intake of breath.

33

Her leg muscles cabled, squeezing her knees tighter until the pressure on his shoulders matched the pressure on his lips. Almost anything would send her over now. He licked her lighter still, his tongue a sheet of silk drawn back and forth across her clit.

He heard her "oh." His ears pricked up. The pressure on his lips was fierce. He kept his licking light and steady. He gripped the fat of her buttocks. Another "oh." Another. He felt the frequency of her moans. Still separate. She wasn't yet inside that space where she would come no matter what he did.

And then she was. Her cries were fast and ragged. He pushed his thumbs into the muscle of her buttocks. He licked her up and down, full on, working her clit like a steamroller. Her body writhed and kicked, her muscles strained, but he refused to be dislodged, clenching her crotch between his head and hands, trapping her legs in the vise of his shoulders and thighs, and still he licked, and licked, and licked. Her crotch burst in his face with a bronco's buck and she screamed and she screamed and her hands were on his head and she was moaning "Thank you, thank you, thank you."

It was over. He raised his head. His chin and cheeks were soaked with her. He struggled up and laid himself on top of her, his upper thigh between her legs, against her soggy sex. He looked down on her face. Her eyes were closed; her mouth was open. Her body heaved to take in air. Her stomach muscles spasmed against his skin in random aftershocks. He wiped his face on hers, smearing her with her juices. His lips were puffy and his head was light. He slumped, his chin against her shoulder, cheek against her cheek. They rested.

"I've missed your mouth," she said, the words traveling an inch to his ear.

"Come back."

"Oh, David. I still feel the pull. I loved to disappear. No wants, no fears. A receptacle. But now I need some room for me. I may not be with Rob forever, but I won't go back to you. I won't be someone's nothing anymore."

"OK." He surprised himself with his calm acceptance. He could argue with "I can't" but not "I won't."

"Want help with that?" she said. His erection was pressed against her thigh. He shook his head. "Then I'd like you to go. I've got a piece to finish."

He stood and silently got dressed. Iris cuddled in upon herself, protecting her breasts and crotch. Her eyes never left him.

"You know my body better than I do," she said. "I'll remember this."

"Madame Ruth's Magic Emporium, potions and notions—you find 'em, we bind 'em."

"It's David."

"Hey, Dave. You're quite the phone fan. But shouldn't you be out wearing women out?"

"I just was. My ex."

"Kink-y. You get lucky?"

He switched the phone to his other ear so he could buzz the window down. A wisp of spring slipped through the car.

"She loved what I did, but she doesn't want me to do it again. Lucky or no?"

"Well, you can make 'em come, but you can't make 'em care,

as my dear departed Henri used to say. You know, I like your voice. But is there some business reason that you called?"

"Yeah. Iris said she'd remember what we did. Is there any truth in that?"

"Sure."

"*Sure?* My partners will remember everything?"

"Of course. I'd like the details, too."

"But Janet at the office! I'll lose my job. She'll sue me into the Stone Age."

"There is a rider—"

"*What?*"

"The Forgetfulness Rider."

"You never said."

"I think it sells better at this point in the client/provider relationship."

There was a long silence.

"I'll bet it does," he said with grudging respect. "You don't miss a trick."

"I'll take that as a compliment."

"What does it give me?"

"Oblivion for others. Anyone you're involved with will find those parts of their day missing from their memory at the stroke of midnight. Only you will remember."

"What does 'involved with' mean exactly?"

"Any contact. You say hi to your neighbor, it's gone. You screw his wife in front of him, it's gone."

"Suppose she tells someone, or puts it in her diary?"

"Gone. Only your memory stays."

"How much?"

"Six hundred."

More silence. "I'll take two."

"That's the spirit. What comes next, so to speak?"

"Food. I feel like I haven't eaten in days."

Her laughter was quick and warm. He hung up.

David entered the mall and bushwhacked his way through the department store. He crossed the crowds on the main thoroughfare and boarded the up escalator. As he moved through the air, he gazed around the multistory atrium at people on the other escalators. He felt like a character in an Escher print.

The third floor held an upscale version of a food court: a mock Italian piazza, lacking only pigeons, lit by large skylights high above. Secretly, he liked it. At the counter of the Blue Parrot, he ordered some lentil soup and an orange Thomasina. He took a small table near the edge of the court.

Light and space dissolved his misgivings from the morning. He was *free*. The Forgetfulness Rider offered pleasure without duty, acts without consequences. Why waste energy with women from his world when he could be with anyone, unfettered by past relationships?

"Your soup, David. With a slug of Inner Beauty, like you like it."

"Hey, Lexi, thanks."

He could have *anyone*. The hum of exhilaration filled his chest. He ate his meal in a rush, hungry to get started. He rounded way up on the tip.

David stood before Beneath It All. The store had always been a no-man's-land for him, filled with garments like teddies and camisoles that only women could name, in shades like ecru and bone that only women could distinguish. But now he had the talisman. He entered for the first time.

He hadn't expected the place to be bustling. How illicit for women to be spending their lunch hours picking out intimate apparel. Would any of them later model her new lingerie for some special person? Or was it born to blush unseen beneath her daily clothes?

He saw a clerk. "Excuse me, where are the changing rooms?"

The clerk looked at David, and at the thong in his hand, and at David again. She manufactured a smile. "To the right, in the back. May I help you?"

"No, thanks. I'll help myself." He felt her eyes follow him as he maneuvered through the aisles of silk and cotton and lace in lavender and cinnamon and deep, deep blue.

There were three saloon doors, side by side. David took a slow breath and fingered the charm. Time to see what this baby could do. "*Avrat taldor.* Come out of the changing room now." There was a long moment's silence. Then the doors opened, and four women emerged.

The first was wearing a loose green robe, but what drew David were her eyes, as splendid as the stars. Beside her was an Asian woman whose breasts were bare, and big for her slight frame. Her hair was cut short, and she wore a bashful smile. A beige bra dangled from her hand. The other two women looked like a couple. Not physically: one was four inches taller and had darker brown hair. But their matching pink push-up bras implied they were still in the rabid-weasel stage of an intimate relationship.

"No need to confine yourself to those small booths," he said.

"Use the whole store for your changing room." The women drifted apart. "And take your time."

David watched. The woman with the starry eyes took off her robe. The lingerie beneath was the color of living flame. The Asian woman put on her bra and looked at herself in a mirror on a pillar. The couple went to the "more for watchers than for wearers" section and laughingly modeled various lacy bras for each other. To David's surprise, another customer joined in, cheerfully trading test bras with the couple as the three complimented one another on their clothes and breasts.

Several clothing changes later, David headed for the front of the store.

"Find what you were looking for?" It was the clerk.

"Yes, thanks." On a whim, he put his hand in his pocket. "Do you wear the store's lingerie?"

"Sure. I get forty percent off."

"*Avrat taldor.* Show me your bra."

The clerk lifted her blouse, and David took in her paisley bra with streaks of silver. "Good. And now below."

She raised her skirt in front. David saw only the soft down of blonde hair.

"You're not wearing any panties."

She smiled sheepishly. "I know. Boyfriend's orders."

"But . . ."

"But if I was, they'd be from here."

Live mannequins. Now that had been more like it. David grinned to himself. What next?

He smelled the chocolate shop from two stores away. Inside,

the aroma was overwhelming. A woman in her thirties with good curved lines in her face and body was meditating on a display case.

"See something you want?"

Her big, wide-set eyes found his face. "Yes. Everything."

"You like chocolate."

"No, I like breathing. I *love* chocolate."

"What'll you get?"

"I can't decide. At these prices, I can only afford one thing. Two things."

"What would you do for all the chocolate you can eat?"

Her smile was quick and bright. "That's an interesting philosophical question."

"Would you emulate Lady Godiva?"

"Lady Godiva had hair down to here."

David looked at the brownish-red hair that wrapped her head in short, tight curls. "Good point. Nevertheless. *Avrat taldor.* Strip naked and tour the mall. When you get back here, there'll be a big box of chocolate waiting for you."

She began to undress.

"Where do you keep your fuck books?"

"Excuse me?" The young woman at the Briar Books information desk looked blankly at David. She had thick black hair that framed her pale face well. Her T-shirt said: IF FRIENDS ASK "HAVE YOU READ THEM ALL?" YOU DON'T OWN ENOUGH BOOKS.

"I want something I can whack off to."

Her cheeks turned pink, and she froze. Then she pointed.

"Our sexuality section is over there, two aisles back, alongside divorce."

"Could you show me, please?"

She looked around nervously for the manager, but he was nowhere in sight. Reluctantly, she stepped out from behind the desk and walked David quickly to the section.

David gestured at the shelves. "You ever read this stuff?"

"I need to get back to help other customers."

"How about this one?" He took down a paperback whose cover displayed a bright red tongue.

"I'll be at the desk if you need any further assistance."

"I do need further assistance. What's your name?"

". . . Alice."

"*Avrat taldor.* Alice, read this." He opened the book and handed it to her, showing where to start. Her gaze flickered over the words for a moment. Her head jerked up. Her eyes were wide.

"Aloud, Alice."

Her face flushed deep red as she dragged her eyes back to the page. She gulped in a breath and began. "'She's on her hands and knees now . . . butt tilted up to get the best of his, of his, his *cock,* to get his cock against the sweet spot in her ass. She puts her hand between her legs and starts to play with her . . . pussy.'"

"You ever had a cock up your ass?"

She shivered and shook her head.

"Read on."

"'She fingers her clit and he moans, he tells her how tight that makes her ass. She puts her finger in her . . . cunt and feels his cock through the wall of her . . . cunt. She presses against his cock and makes him moan again. She's really worked up now. She wants to come with a, with a hard cock up her ass, to feel her ass contract around a hard cock. Like all the other times tonight.'"

"Tell me, you ever think about being fucked by a lot of guys in a row?"

She blushed more deeply, which he wouldn't have thought possible. Her nod was almost imperceptible.

"You have any books like this at home?"

She let out a sigh, and her shoulders relaxed. She looked into his face for the first time. "Yes."

"What's your favorite?"

"See Sis Suck." Her cheeks were aflame, but her voice was steady.

"And what's your favorite here?"

Alice smiled in surprise. She beckoned almost coyly, and led him to the poetry section, where she took a book off the shelves. She read: "'O Western wind, when wilt thou blow, / That the small rain down can rain? / Christ, that my love were in my arms / And I in my bed again!'"

"Beautiful." He meant her passion as much as the poem.

"Isn't it? It's lasted half a thousand years. I fell in love with that poem when I was twelve, and now I love it more."

David couldn't help but smile himself. He weighed his options. Move on, or spend more time with her? Both. "You know any other hot women at this mall?"

Alice's face colored on cue. "Well, my friend Sukey's gorgeous. She does hair at Gnomon."

"Take me there."

*   *   *

Gnomon Styling was a small salon, with half a dozen seats. A woman met them as they entered, her face lighting up. "Alice, honey. It is good to see you again. And so soon—is your hair misbehaving itself? But no, it is splendid."

This must be Sukey. David agreed with Alice's assessment. Sukey's cheekbones, sitting high in a serene and regal face, promised she would be more beautiful at sixty.

"Thanks to you. Sukey, this is David."

He took the offered hand. "You cut her hair?"

"Yes, sir. Good hair. Thick. Alive."

"Yes. Yes, I can see that. You do good work." An idea came to David. "I think she needs more styling."

"But she was here just two days ago. All is OK."

"Not all." He walked Alice to a chair by a sink, and Sukey followed. "Alice, lift your skirt."

"Sir! She is a lady. Alice!"

"And take those off."

"Alice!"

Alice placed her panties on David's palm. Her face was only mildly pink, as if her blushing muscles had worn out. He gestured, and she raised her skirt high.

He turned to Sukey. "*Avrat taldor.*" He indicated the thick patch of black that Alice had revealed. "Look, there. She needs your skills. Trim her." He nodded to Alice. "Sit down and make yourself accessible."

Alice positioned herself gingerly on the plastic seat. David heard a murmur from behind. Two women had entered the salon. Alice leaned backward, sliding her buttocks to the edge of the seat, and the chair leaned back with her. She slowly raised her legs, then spread them and hooked her knees over the chair arms. David took in a breath. Alice closed her eyes.

Sukey gazed at her friend. "Miss Alice. What is your pleasure?"

"Oh, Sue. I've no idea. Use your judgment."

Sukey considered. She picked up a light pink bottle and used it to mist the hair between Alice's legs. Alice shivered.

Sukey took a pair of scissors from the counter and knelt carefully on the floor between Alice's legs. Her scissors clicked happily as she layered the longer strands. "So rich."

David watched from the side. The new women were now beside him, also watching.

Sukey leaned closer to see clearer, the tips of her scissors dancing just above the skin. Sukey's breath drifted onto Alice. David saw the skin roughen, the mounds at the roots of the hairs erecting like hundreds of tiny nipples. And he smelled Alice— very strongly. He breathed her in like opium. The woman next to him slid her hand inside her pants.

Sukey switched to an electric razor. She placed a palm lightly on Alice's thigh and pressed sideways to smooth the skin and make the bushy hair stand up straight. She trimmed the edges, creating a crisp outline. Then the razor buzzed in the center, thinning the overhang, discovering, exposing.

David realized that Alice had opened her eyes. She was staring at herself in the mirror, staring at the woman who was spread wide open. Staring and staring and staring.

Sukey was staring, too. She slowly sunk her head and took one long lick. She stood. She gave Alice a hand mirror. "OK, that is good. See now how graceful, like a frame."

Alice painstakingly examined the world between her legs,

the tilting mirror flicking echoes of the overhead lights around the room. "It's beautiful."

David's work here was done. He headed for the door.

"Style me next."

"No, me."

"Skip the scissors, honey—all I need is the tongue."

"Excuse me, where are the urinals?"

"Next door. This is the women's room." She was washing her hands.

"That explains it." David crossed the glossy black tiles to the next sink. He faced the wide wall mirror and unzipped his fly. No point in having power if you don't abuse it.

"What the hell are you doing?"

"Pissing in the sink. This is how *I* spell relief. Mm, gotta cut back on the Pepsi."

"Jesus. Get out!"

She made shooing motions, speckling David's shirt with water.

"Sasha, what's going on?" The question came from the stalls.

David gunned the tap and sent a stream of water at Sasha. She stumbled backward. "There's a crazy out here, Cait."

Cait opened the stall door. Like Sasha, she was lithe and twentyish. "It's a guy!"

"No need to fight." David waggled his penis. "Take turns."

"Sasha, your shirt is soaking wet."

It was, and it was abundantly clear that she wore nothing underneath. David enjoyed the view. So go with it. "*Avrat taldor.* Cait, get your shirt good and wet, too. You and Sasha wait here until everyone arrives. Then join them."

And David was out the door, zipping his fly as he went. He moved quickly through the crowds, scanning for braless women. He charmed half a dozen, telling each, "Wet T-shirt contest in the women's room next to Fuchsia Shock. You'll be competing. Go there and prepare." Then he impaneled judges from the men among the crowd, and sent them off after the women.

Suits You. Feet First. Sofa So Good. The stores drifted by as David ambled along. He basked in a vision of the whole mall humming with horniness, and all because of him.

The Downpour Store. On the Wall. My Tie. Panache Jewelry. What to do next? He waited for inspiration. Wheat and Wine, Tofu Town, Fleurs du Mall.

The Allegretto Day Spa. He looked through its wall of glass. A woman was tilted back in one of several reclining seats. She had long gray hair streaked with white, and her eyes were covered with cotton pads. A short, plump woman with a round face highlighted by pitch-black eyebrows was swathing white goop onto the streak-haired woman's face with what looked like a large popsicle stick.

David walked in, passing shelves of neatly stacked cosmetics and soaps. A woman with a trim body and a cheerful smile walked over. "Good afternoon, I'm Stellina. Welcome to my shop. What can we do for you, sir?"

"Could you tell me what that woman's getting?"

"A collagen facial. For DNA reparation of the upper skin layers."

"Collagen?"

"It's a gelatin made from extracellular proteins. It helps your skin retain its natural elasticity."

"I like the idea of a protein facial."

"An excellent choice. I can set you up with Amy as soon as she finishes with Miss Chaplin here."

"I mean, I like the idea for you."

Stellina looked a little confused, but no less cheerful. "I don't think I follow you, sir."

"*Avrat taldor.* Have a seat over there, by the window. Amy, please provide Stellina with some eye pads."

David stepped out into the mall proper and scanned the passersby. He saw a group of teenage boys in black T-shirts and oversize jeans. He walked over and made his pitch. The boys looked at one another. One boy, clearly the leader, quizzed David with irritation and excitement. David brought them to the window of the store. Stellina was reclining placidly in her seat. The lead boy addressed his group. "In line, one at a time, no pushing. Let's go."

The boy turned and walked into the store without waiting for acknowledgment. His posse trailed behind him. David watched through the window. The boy strode to Stellina. He loosed his belt with one sharp motion, opened his jeans, and downed his zipper in a graceful flurry. With a yank, his jeans and shorts were below his buttocks. His erection, now freed, catapulted upward and slapped against his belly. It came to rest at a steep angle, pointing toward the ceiling and viciously hard. David sighed with a mixture of memory and desire: to be seventeen again.

The boy crowded next to Stellina's head. He made a fist at waist level and started moving his hips, fucking his fist, the head of his uncircumcised penis disappearing then reappearing inches from Stellina's oblivious face. David had barely time to notice the boy was left-handed when the pistoning penis discharged streams of semen across Stellina's face. Her mouth formed an O of surprise, then relaxed. The semen graced her cheeks in broken lines resembling an I Ching toss. The masturbation had taken less than thirty seconds.

The leader hitched up his jeans but didn't rebelt them. He sauntered to the back of the line. The next boy was already beside Stellina's head, slapping his penis against her sticky cheek to get himself hard. The other boys strained to see. One of them had released his penis, tugging on it as it stuck out through his fly. But no one left the line or jostled—they complied like a cadet corps.

David felt the press of bodies around him, and realized that others were watching the show through the glass. His show. He worked his way out of the crowd.

Now for some souvenirs of his trip. David entered You Are a Camera and went past the checkout counter to the back of the store, where the equipment was sold. He called out, "I've got a photography assignment for people who know how to shoot." Several customers gathered around.

He turned to the goateed young man behind the counter. "Please outfit each of these people with a decent camera and two rolls of fast color film. We'll get the equipment back to you later today. Put it on my card."

David charmed the volunteers, then huddled with them. He told them where he'd been, what he wanted them to capture on film, and where to take the film when they were done. His camera crew left the store and scattered.

*　　　*　　　*

The witch's number was still busy. David, waiting for the mall elevator, thumbed off his phone in irritation. How dare she talk with other men.

That made him think of Rob. Then Iris. Iris on her bed. Her taste. He felt her clit hard beneath his tongue, her knees clamped around his shoulders.

"Going down?"

David started. The elevator door was open. Inside was a tall, lean woman, maybe fifty, maybe a little more.

"Sorry." He stepped in.

Why still stuck on Iris? He shifted to the mall scenes, but none was near as strong. What he'd called power now felt petty. He realized he hadn't touched one person here, and shook his head. His day was getting away from him. He'd tried to treat sex as a game, but after playing at this mall for hours, all he'd won was an occasional erection.

"Hey, things can't be that hard."

He looked at the woman and found her looking back with a directness that unsettled him. Her face was angular, with dark gray eyes, a small nose, and a wide mouth. Her hair was short and intentionally uneven, blonde with scattered streaks of blonder blonde.

He realized his fists were clenched. He consciously relaxed them. "I'm OK. My plans aren't working out, that's all."

"Maybe you should plan less."

The doors slid open, revealing the underground parking garage. The woman exited the elevator. David watched her walk.

He felt his magic moments flying by. Frustration mixed with desperation. "You. Wait."

The woman paused.

He thrust his hand into his pocket, gripped the charm, and said in a loud, clear voice, "*Avrat taldor.* Make it all OK. Satisfy me."

The woman turned slowly. Her gaze was strong and serious. What had he done? Her face broke into a wicked grin. "I'm Priscilla. I'll be your server today."

He stumbled into her apartment, led inexorably by her grip on his erection. She had brought him to her car, insisted he expose his penis, and driven the ten minutes to her place with only one hand on the wheel, which had been fine with him, until she parked, when she refused to let go and instead firmly guided him across the front seat, out the driver's door, across the small sunlit backyard, through the back entrance, and up a flight of stairs to her place.

She bolted the door behind them and let go at last. He was panting like he'd run for miles. She started taking off her clothes. "Come on, hard guy, I'm game to go." Her breasts were small and firm, set well apart. Her arms were muscled. A moment later, he glimpsed her pert behind as she left the room. He tore at the buttons on his shirt, then stripped off his pants. He went after her.

The door led to a small room dominated by a huge bed. The walls were lined with bookcases full of books, with more books piled on top, and still more books in heaps across the hardwood floor. They made a cordial disorder that seemed to have some deeper pattern. But all David really saw was Priscilla.

She had planted herself in the center of the bed, flat on her back. Her legs were in the air, straight and spread wide, making an obscene V. She had a hand between her legs, coyly covering herself. "Come and get it."

He was on the bed in a flash, his erection leading the way. He crawled to her, then over her, his penis knocking against the back of her hand. "I'm ready when you are."

"Then what the fuck are you doing up here?" Her hand shot to his hair and grabbed tight. She forced his head down and away, making him crawl backward until his face was inches above her vulva. "Pussy, meet David." She pulled his head down, jamming his face into her wetness. "David, pussy."

He inhaled her liquid. He snorted thickly and tried to jerk his head away, but her grip did not relax a bit. For an instant, he feared he would drown. Then he discovered he could breathe through the corners of his mouth. He took in tiny breaths. His nose cleared.

"Enough lollygagging. Get to work."

She let go of his hair, freeing him to move where she wanted. Her legs came down and wrapped around his neck and shoulders, pinning him. His arms lay silent at his sides, barely giving him support. A humming in his head replaced the usual cacophony of thoughts.

"Eat."

Her clitoris was erect and long, like a miniature penis. He pursed his lips around it and sucked, a baby on a teat. He felt like she was feeding him. A wave of gratitude took him by surprise.

"Uh-huh. That's good. Uh-huh . . . Give me some tongue, pussy boy."

He had no idea what kind of licking she wanted, so he tried it all. Soft, fast, slide, slow, pump, liquid, fierce, a dozen variations on the dance.

"Like that . . . lighter."

He followed her words and the muscles in her thighs.

"Yeah. Higher and to the right . . . my right. *There.* Fuck, you're good. I knew you'd be good."

Her pulse was throbbing in her clit. He sucked in time, then off time, speeding up, rushing her.

"Oh, yeah. Oh, yeah."

He was alternating sucking and licking. Sometimes he nipped.

"That's good. That. Is. Good." She lifted her buttocks off the bed and flexed her legs repeatedly, humping his face. "Good, good, good—" Her fists were thumping on his shoulders and occasionally his head. "—good, *good, good, good, stop!*" Her legs uncoiled and she pushed his head hard. She was out from under him, and he went face-first into the bedspread. He lay there quiet, calm, confused, undone.

"Hey, honey pie, don't fall asleep. Good start, but I'm just getting cranked."

David lifted his head. Priscilla was on her knees, breasts, and cheek, her arms outstretched on the bed above her head. Her back was strongly arched, ending in the heart-stopping curve of her buttocks. It was an intensely inviting image.

Slowly, dreamily, he raised himself off the bed and knelt behind her. He brought his penis tentatively to her undefended lips. He thought of Iris, earlier today.

"Other hole, stud. There's lube under the pillow."

He felt foolish, and the inevitable rush of anger followed close behind. She was the enemy. Except, she wasn't. How strange. He rooted around and retrieved the small black bottle, flipped up the spout, and squeezed out some liquid. His finger found her anus.

She sighed. "That's right. In you go. Yessss . . . yeah. Oh, yeah. More lube . . . that's good . . . Uh-huh . . . Another one. There. Pre-stretch me. Work my ass . . . Yeah. One more to grow on . . . Fuck, that's good. If I had time, I'd take your whole hand up my hole. I'll settle for your dick."

David lubricated his hard penis. He put the tip at her anus and stopped, unsure.

"Cat got your cock?" She gave herself a spank. "Shove it in."

He nudged, and the head of his penis popped through the ring of muscle. The rest of him followed easily till he was balls deep in her. She was warm. And snug.

She groaned. "Oh, yeah. Nice and full. Bet that looks hot." She reached back and spread her buttocks, exposing her anus stretched around his erection.

He slowly pulled out, watching his penis get longer and longer and still longer, like a dozen clowns getting out of a tiny car. He stopped when he could see the ridge below the penis head. He crawled back in, watching himself disappear inside her. Another slow stroke. And another. Hypnotic.

He pulled all the way out. Her anus stayed open, remembering his penis.

"Cunt teaser."

He flicked his hips and reentered.

She gasped. "Oh, yeah, that's hot. My hole is all relaxed." She let go of her buttocks and the flesh cuddled around him. He moved more quickly. "*Yes.* That's right. Fuck me. Fuck me. Fuck. Me. Fuck. Me. Fuck . . ."

He thrust in time with her chant, pushing her face into the bed. There was a buzzing round his penis, and he realized she'd pressed a massage vibrator against her crotch.

"Fuck. Me. Ram me. *Take* me. Come on, pussy boy. Harder. Uh. You can do better than that. Uh. Yes. UH. Fuck!"

He pounded away, gripping her hips to anchor her. His balls were beating against her lips, sometimes getting buzzed by the vibrator. Her voice's volume grew, but now her words were indistinct. She was sucking on a bright red dildo.

She turned the vibrator up a notch, bathing his penis in sensation. Her muscles contracted around him. He fought to stave off orgasm, desperate not to come too soon. She met his thrusts with back thrusts of her own. Her buttocks quivered. She came, growling deep within her throat as her rectum fluttered around his penis. She jerked away, leaving him on his knees having intercourse with the air.

She rolled onto her back, looked up at him, and grinned. "Nice hard-on. Or are you just happy to see me?"

"I want you." He did. Terribly.

"I can see that. How sweet."

"Please."

"Lie down."

"But . . ."

"Shut up. Lie down."

He lay down.

She straddled his waist, crouching, the soles of her feet on the bed. She eased herself down, balancing with her hands, until her buttocks met his penis. She used one hand to brace herself on his leg, the other to guide him to her anus. She tucked him in and lowered herself his full length.

He groaned.

"Welcome back." She started moving, back straight, up and down. It felt fabulous to him. She raised her arms carefully, keeping herself balanced, and clasped her hands behind her neck. She moved on him, her calf muscles straining. He gazed up at her in awe, drinking in her breasts and belly. She smiled triumphantly. He caught a flash of his penis between her legs.

"Like me jerking you off with my asshole?"

"*Yes.*"

Her leg muscles were shaking, and she sank down to her knees, putting her hands on the bed alongside him. She rode him slowly. It *did* feel like masturbation, her rectum a perfect fist: warm, smooth, formfitting, each movement rubbing everything.

She leaned forward, dangling her breasts above him. He lifted his head and took a nipple in his mouth. He sucked; it grew. He mouthed the other nipple. Tantalus released.

She lowered her breasts onto his chest, nipples poking. She put her mouth on his. Her lips were parted, and he matched them. She held the kiss. Their breathing synchronized, and he inhaled warm moist air. She was moving on his erection, clinging, clutching, pulling him closer. Her tongue wandered into his mouth. He met it, embraced it, and followed it home. When was the last time that he'd really kissed?

She rose to her knees and leaned back a little, still riding him, but more slowly. She ran her hand gently through her pubic hair. She tapped her clitoris. She pushed two fingers up inside her vagina.

"I feel you." Her fingers traced his penis through her inner wall. It jumped. "Down, boy. Not yet."

Eric Albert

She took her fingers out and turned them slowly near his face, showing how they glistened. She moved them to her center, spreading her lips with her other hand, and started masturbating, her fingers an upside-down V around her clitoris.

She hunched up and down on his erection, short stroke following short stroke, each ending with a grind against his crotch, her buttocks rubbing his balls. Dirty words stuttered out of her.

She started coming, wetting his crotch. He pushed up into her, straining for release. She kept on coming, and he got wetter. A rank smell reached his nose. She saw his face and laughed. "That's my pissy boy."

His hand leapt high and slapped her cheek.

She slapped him back.

He thrust up his pelvis and bucked her off, her urine flying to spatter the bedspread. He scrambled to his knees. She'd landed on her side. He reached for her, but she rolled quicker. He snagged her leg; she kicked herself loose. They both rose to their knees. For a moment, they were still. She grinned and showed her teeth. He was conscious of his penis jutting out. He shambled toward her on his knees, the mattress sinking beneath him. Her arms were out, ready to parry. He lunged and caught her wrist. She twisted back against his thumb, forcing her release, and slapped his hard-on with her other hand. He roared and launched himself full at her. His shoulder hit her chest and she went over backward. He went with her. She struggled to slide out from underneath but couldn't budge him. She grabbed his hair with both fists and pulled. He clamped his hands around her wrists and squeezed until her grip went slack. He pushed her hands back to the bed, beside her head. It took more effort than he'd thought. He had her pinned.

56

He started laughing and he couldn't stop. Then he stopped trying to stop, and let the laughter come without reserve. So rare a thing, this loss of control. So frightening; so good. And she was laughing, too.

He caught up with his body: his breath was rasping in his throat; his muscles quaked; his skin was stuck to hers with sweat and urine; his penis was a log between them.

He waited until his breathing slowed. He cautiously brought his body up off hers, keeping her pinned. He positioned his knees on her upper arms, then put his weight there. He let go of her hands.

He looked down at her, past his erection. Her face was an honest fifty, the skin smooth but no longer creamy. Her smile was broad and sweet. Her eyes were deep, and he felt himself dissolving.

He shook his head to clear his thoughts. He pushed a pillow underneath her head. "Stick out your tongue, bitch."

She giggled, then did what he said. He settled lower till his penis touched.

"Lick me clean."

She licked along the underside, using the flat of her tongue. He shifted forward, and she licked up to his hair.

"Taste it. Your lube, your ass, your piss."

Her tongue was busy. Back and forth, round and round.

"Yes, that, up near the head . . . a little to the left. Yes. Right there. That. Do that."

He lapsed into silence, focused on the feeling from her tongue. Her licks were light, almost teasing, but she patiently kept on the right spot, a flash of heaven with each lick. His penis tensed, nodding gently over her tongue.

His hands were on the front of his thighs, and he realized his grip was tight. He noticed muscles in his shoulders, back, and buttocks. He ached to push his penis into her, any hole, and let loose all his pent-up pressure in her body. But he also loved this delicate, torturous pleasure, his whole body like a statue except the quarter inch of his penis that was vibrantly alive.

She licked.

His penis quivered like a divining rod over a river.

She licked.

Yes.

"Take it."

She was already pulling her head back and opening her mouth. He put his penis in and her lips closed around him. Her tongue was swirling perfectly, the single point of pleasure turning white hot as his penis shot its load. She took it all and kept on licking.

His face was red. His balls were empty. He tumbled off her, coming to rest on his back. She was on him in a second, her face right above his. She grinned wide and let his semen fall to splash upon his face. She kissed him fiercely. He kissed back.

Five minutes later, he was on the other side of the apartment door. He sat on the floor and put on his socks and shoes, then walked slowly down the front stairway and out the front door.

It was now past six, but the sky was still full of light. He loved how spring days went on forever. The air was rich and sweet, and his lips still tasted Priscilla's kiss. Happiness welled up inside him. Why not call the witch and share it?

But first things first: get the car. He walked a few blocks to the commuter train stop and grabbed a taxi back to the mall. He stopped inside for a minute, then took the elevator down to the basement garage. He'd seen no sign that the scenes he'd started were still going on. Next things next: a shower. His health club was just half a mile away.

He stashed his clothing in his locker. Was it safe to leave the charm? He transferred it to the tiny pocket of his bathing trunks, and went into the shower room. Chrome fixtures were evenly spaced along the far wall. A twist of a knob and he was flooded with hot water. It was delicious, religious. At first, it cleansed his surface. Sweat, semen, urine—all gone with the deluge, until his skin was naked.

He twisted the knob some more. The water was scalding. Now deeper things were washed away: fatigue within his muscles, an ache inside his bones. The water seemed to enter and go streaming through his veins.

The last to leave was intellect. He stood untethered from his day, from his thoughts, from himself. And yet, he felt connected, deeply connected, to . . . something. With everything gone, there was space for the world.

Two men entered from the locker room. They were in their forties: some gray in the beard of one, some sag in the other's stomach. They nodded to David and chose adjacent showers down the wall. They needled each other and laughed as water cascaded off their receding hairlines.

A vision flared up, like a match head at ignition: David realized he could make them fuck each other. Or take turns sucking him. Or . . . he tilted back his head and let the water pound his face.

When he opened his eyes, the men were gone.

He donned his trunks and exited to the pool room. The fluorescent light, the chlorine fumes—it always felt unreal, but never more fantastical than now. The pool was huge and almost unpopulated. The leftmost lane, his favorite, was free. He stood at the edge of the pool, adjusted his goggles, and dove.

The instantaneous transfer from the world of air to the world of water took his breath away. He glided, letting his momentum take him a third of the length. He felt that he could stay beneath forever. When his motion slowed, he used his arms and legs to move himself along the lane. His fingers touched the far wall, and he surfaced.

He swam laps diligently, keeping his face down in the water, his eyes open behind the goggles. He was eager to stay in this separate realm, and he raised his head only when his lungs insisted. Whatever thoughts occurred to him went trailing in his wake.

Fifteen minutes was enough. He pulled himself up onto the rough concrete side and felt the world's weight settle on him once again. He bore it more lightly now.

Lunch seemed like a long time ago. He needed to clean the chlorine off, then get some food. He took a step toward the men's shower room and paused. He turned and used the other door instead.

To his right, a massive woman was under a shower, soaping herself. He gaped. He had never seen such large breasts in real life. If average breasts could hold a pencil underneath, hers could trap an arm. Her stomach hid her crotch. Her arms were thicker than his thighs.

She smiled warmly at him. "Wrong room, stranger. Next door thataway."

He groped for the pocket on his trunks and found the charm. "*Avrat taldor.* Uh, keep showering."

The woman smiled again. "My pleasure. Hear that, Dorothy? The nice man likes me washing."

"Me, too. It's cleanliness next to godliness."

David realized there was a woman beside her. Other details of the room developed. Like the men's, it had a wall of showers, a facing wall of sinks topped with a long mirror, a wooden bench along one side, and low overhead lighting glimmering off a tiled floor. There were some differences: a wall-mounted hair dryer by each sink; tiles colored red, not black. And naked women under the showers.

The enormous woman started rinsing, using both hands to lift a breast into the spray. David moved so he could get a look at her companion. Dorothy had a button nose and a smart smile. In any other context, he would have said she had full breasts. The rest of her was small, and it would take two of her, maybe two and a half, to make up her friend.

Her friend held out a hand. "I'm Martha. I didn't catch your name."

He shook. "David." Her hand was wet, and drops from her shower sprinkled his arm.

"The godly one is Dorothy."

David and Dorothy nodded at each other.

Size wasn't the only thing that distinguished the women. Dorothy's hair hung loosely down to her shoulders; Martha's was regimented in cornrows. Martha's skin was dark and creamy as chocolate mousse; Dorothy had a CPA's tan.

Martha gestured to her glistening body. "I don't believe I can get much cleaner than this."

"Then do something with Dorothy."

"Did you have anything in mind?"

". . . No. Use your imagination."

Martha raised an eyebrow, then grinned. She moved next to Dorothy, who, though dwarfed in mass, was a few inches taller.

"Hey, don't hog my shower."

"Wanna arm-wrestle for it?" Martha flexed biceps that could halt a charging yak.

"Nah, let's boob-wrestle." Dorothy turned and grabbed a large nipple with each hand.

Martha let out a loud moan and half collapsed, her back supported by the wall. "Cheater."

"All's fair. I guess your titties haven't changed since college."

"That was a hundred years ago. You swore you'd never tell."

"Sue me. But first . . ." Dorothy kissed Martha, and kept on kissing her. Martha groaned, her sounds muffled by Dorothy's lips, her nipples gripped by Dorothy's fingers. Hot water rained down.

Dorothy broke the kiss. "You taste so good." She was panting.

"Why, so do you, honey."

"I still remember how you taste down there."

"Shh. You'll make me blush."

Dorothy glanced over her shoulder at David. "I'm going to suck her nipples. It makes her crazy." She put her hands under Martha's breast and tilted it up. She dipped her head and took the nipple in her mouth. Martha's head banged back against the wall and her mouth opened wide. David watched her expressions ebb and flow. He could tell when the sucking got stronger, when Dorothy bit her, and when the orgasm hit her like an avalanche.

Martha staggered out of the shower, pushing Dorothy aside like tinsel, and stopped in front of David. "That was bracing. I thank you kindly."

"Have him join us," said Dorothy.

"An excellent thought." Martha put her hands softly on his shoulders. "Come on, David. Let the monkey out of the bag." He tried to step backward, but couldn't move an inch.

Dorothy scurried over, crouched, and yanked down his trunks. His penis appeared before her eyes. "So cute! But shouldn't it be a bit more . . . interested?"

David's face felt like fire. Martha looked down. "He's just shy. Why don't you make him feel more welcome?"

Dorothy skittered her hands over his balls, then up and down his penis, speckling him with finger kisses. She wrapped her fist firmly around his penis. She tugged several times, stretching him. When she unclasped her hand, he was still limp. She ducked her head and put his penis in her mouth. She licked and sucked, gently at first, then more strongly. She rubbed his balls at the same time. She let him slide out of her mouth. His penis hung down, slick with her saliva, a little longer and a quarter hard. Dorothy shook her head.

David realized Martha's grip had loosened. He turned and almost tripped, his ankles bound together by his bathing trunks. He dragged them up and raced out of the room. He heard their laughter billowing behind him.

He hurried along the side of the pool and stepped into the men's shower room. No one was there. He continued through, into the locker room. A tall, thin man was sitting on a bench in front of a row of lockers, putting on his socks. David charmed him and moved on. There was no one in the next aisle of lockers, but the third aisle held three men. They looked to be in their late twenties, and they clearly knew where the weight room was. One had a small ponytail. David charmed them and headed back to the women's locker room, the four men in tow.

"These women want cock, so give them plenty of it. Dorothy, Martha—do anything they say."

As David headed for the privacy of the men's locker room, the men shucked their clothing like it was radioactive. There was nothing wrong with their erections.

"Ye Olde Sorcery Shoppe—sit down for a spell."

"It's David."

"Hey, Dave. How's it hanging?"

"Things suck."

"I'll just bet you mean that in some kind of negative way."

"I can't get it up."

"Can't get enough? You've got a frigging Charm of Power."

"Up. I can't get it *up*. An erection."

"An infection? With the STD Rider? Let me check the refund policy."

"Screw the STD Rider. *I can't get hard!*"

"Dave, you can't have said what I just heard. Go somewhere with a better signal."

He cursed and moved from the men's locker room into the hall. He lowered his voice. "My. Penis. Stays. Limp."

"Ah. Eyes bigger than your dick, eh? How many times you get your gun today?"

Janet. Iris. Priscilla. "Three."

"Jerk off this morning or last night?"

"Last night. Twice."

"Busy, busy. Can you normally come more than five times in twenty-four hours?"

"How the hell should I know?"

"I'll take that as a no. Looks like you've found your limit. Not to worry—your hard-on will be back tomorrow."

"But the charm runs out at midnight."

"I hate it when that happens. Though there is another option. . . ."

David closed his eyes. "How much."

"Four hundred dollars gets you a Potency Pack, good for up to three rock-hard erections and accompanying ejaculations."

"Three?"

"It's a marketing thing. Unless you want the ten-pack."

"*No.*"

"Then three it is. This used to be my biggest seller. Then Viagra came along and kicked that all to shit."

He wondered just how many customers she had. "Who buys it now?"

"The folks who haven't planned ahead. Amyl nitrite fans. Guys who want the associated Soreness-Protection Rider."

"You didn't—"

"I'll throw it in for free. You've earned it. Here's how you use the pack. . . ."

David reentered the women's shower room with more men and looked around.

Martha was on her back in the middle of the damp floor. The tall man was kneeling at her side, across from the man with the ponytail. Each of them was pumping his erection into the tight, warm space beneath a bulky breast.

The other two weight-room men were standing in front of a sink, taking Dorothy's mouth and vagina. They had her in the air at waist level, holding her by hips and shoulders. She was clasping the buttocks of the forward man to hold herself steady. Her breasts, hanging down like udders, echoed the thrusts from front and rear.

A stout woman David hadn't seen before was sitting on the long bench, her legs spread and stiff. She was vigorously rubbing her almost-hairless crotch. Her gaze switched between the trios like a spectator at a tennis match.

The new men filtered in. David ducked into the women's locker room and yelled "*Avrat taldor.* Come to the showers."

As he returned, a teenage boy was settling himself on the floor between the bench woman's legs. He moved her hands away and put his mouth where they'd been. She smiled tenderly at him, then went back to watching.

Dorothy was coughing, and David turned to look. The penis in her mouth was shooting, and she couldn't swallow fast enough. The man behind was ramming her, which didn't help. Now he was coming, too, pressed deep as he could get inside her.

Women, some half dressed, some less, walked in. The room was getting crowded. David called, "Act out your filthy fantasies." The swirl of flesh was dizzying as people went for what they wanted in a confusion of motion.

He muttered the new sentence that the witch had given him. He flicked his uncooperative penis with his index finger. He instantly was hard—bone hard, stalagmite hard—as if an iron rod had been implanted in his crotch. He touched it wonderingly. He looked around.

Two new men were masturbating using Martha's breasts. Her legs were splayed and bent, her feet flat on the tile. Between them, Dorothy crouched, her arm at Martha's opening and all her hand inside. Dorothy moved her arm forward and back, and Martha moaned.

One man grunted and pulled out from Martha's breast. A bald man in his sixties darted forward, pushed the breast aside, and lapped the sticky liquid underneath. When he had gotten all of it, he sat back on his haunches, waiting for the second man to finish. Dorothy was focused on her fist in Martha, and barely noticed when a paunchy man got down behind and guided his long erection into her.

Some people were dragging exercise mats into the room. Others wadded up towels to kneel on. Above the room's groans and cries, a woman's wail rang out. "My ass. *Please*, someone screw my ass." David headed toward the voice. He maneuvered around a woman who was furiously riding a man, her breasts jouncing, and almost stepped on a man who was facedown on the floor, humping the tiles while squeezing his own buttocks. Nearby, a man yanked off a woman's bra and stuffed it in her mouth.

The wailing woman was on her back, her head in the lap of a man who held her ankles near his shoulders. Her legs were spread above her, her backside off the floor. A man was going at her, with two more at the ready. David joined the line.

"*Screw* my ass. Yeah, do it, do it."

The man inside her shook and shot. The next man took his place. A few feet to David's right, along the shower wall, half a dozen men were standing side by side. Two women knelt before them, giving service with their mouths. The women seemed to be competing with each other.

"Yeah, do it. *Screw me*."

David's attention returned to the woman on the floor. The man inside her galloped to his finish. The next was in and out in thirty seconds. David knelt.

The woman's anus was gaping open. He put his penis near it, hunched forward, and was in. Her anal muscle all relaxed, her rectum full of semen—it might as well have been her other hole.

She gasped. "Oh, that's a hard one. Screw me to the floor."

He did his best, wielding his erection like a weapon and stabbing her deeply, again and again.

"Do it, screw me, screw my ass."

He gave it all he had. His balls banged so hard against her buttocks that his whole groin ached.

"Come on, come on."

He came.

"Another dick. I need another." The woman looked up through her legs, meeting the eyes of the man holding her open. "Am I doing good, honey?"

David withdrew from the woman and rose slowly to his feet. Being a character in someone else's fantasy was disenchanting. Four new men were now in line. David turned away.

The woman on the bench still had the boy between her legs. Beside her sat two men who were in their mid-twenties. Their dark eyes and curly hair matched; they had to be brothers. They were watching the room. Each had a hand on the other's penis.

A woman, sitting cross-legged on a mat, was spanking a large hairy man who sprawled across her lap. Three men and a woman awaited their turn beneath her palm.

A girl was lying on her back, her long brown hair streaming on the floor. She looked like a younger Iris, and David felt his heartbeat quicken. Her knees were hugged against her breasts. Her eyes were closed. Her vagina was open and leaking semen. One of the weight lifters, hard again, knelt in front of her and slid himself inside. She smiled. Her eyes stayed closed.

David's searching eyes found Martha. She looked like Gulliver brought down by Lilliput. A small man with a large penis was straddling her face, moving his member in her mouth. She had a penis in each hand; the men attached were using her fists for intercourse. Two other men were at her sides, their penises sliding beneath her breasts. And Dorothy, her eyes and buttocks glazed, now had both hands in her old roommate.

David squatted on the floor beside Martha's head and flicked his penis, which sprang up like a tiger. He could smell the small man's sweat and feel his heat. David began to masturbate, moving his hand leisurely up and down his hyper-stiff erection. His other hand caressed his balls. He watched the small man use Martha's mouth, and matched strokes with him. Soon David was on the verge. He kept himself there with gentle touches, watching, waiting. The small man hissed as his penis pulsed in Martha's mouth. David squeezed himself and his semen burst out, splattering against the man's chest, then dripping down to Martha's chin. David's eyes met Martha's. She swallowed lustily and winked.

"Black magic woman—let me make a devil out of you."

"It's David."

"I know, I've grown accustomed to your voice. What's up, besides your revitalized dick?"

"I don't know. I'm not sure why I'm calling."

"How many guesses do I get?"

"I'm sorry; it's not really business."

"Oh, what the hell. It's quiet here. No play, all work makes Jill a jerk."

"I don't . . . I thought . . . I was in this room of people, and everyone was having sex, and I was watching, even joining in, and it was . . . friendly. Warm. But not hot. I'm living out a fantasy, but it feels like nothing special."

"Pain in the ass."

"Yeah. And all those people . . . you know, I masturbate a lot, but that's not lonely. This was lonely. I don't know what to do."

"Stay away from orgies?"

"I'll think about it. Right now, I'm feeling empty. Got anything to help? Some potion, pill, or powder?"

"Nope."

"You must have one more rider that you're dying to unload."

"Dave, if something worked for that, *I'd* take it." Her voice was serious.

"So what do people do?"

"Work. Love. Exercise."

"That's so damn hard."

"Life's a bitch, and then you die. Well, not me personally, but you know what I mean."

"You ever feel like this?"

"Just every frigging day. My clients aren't so happy to start with. And then they learn that I can't sell them what they really need."

"That sucks."

"Indeed it does. The world is full of emptiness; without it there'd be nothing left."

"Who said that?"

"Richard, my first lover, may he rest in peace. It's stuck with me. Hey, when did you last eat?"

"One, give or take."

"It's half-past nine, Dave. Nice to know we share this angst, but there's another reason you're feeling empty."

The witch was right: he was starving. Knowing that helped, and his spirits rose as he steered into the Square. A parking space emptied just ahead of him, a sight so rare he wondered for a moment if the charm had deeper powers. No, even magic had its limits.

The waitress smiled and greeted him. There were a dozen restaurants that knew him well. He liked being part of café society, even if his society had a membership of one.

She seated him in the back room without being asked. It was dark and intimate, and he felt at home, more at home than he did in his apartment. This had once been someone's house, so maybe that made sense. He glanced at the menu, then looked around: the usual mix of professors, students, and loners. Most had been born in some other country, and half weren't speaking English.

The waitress returned and took his order: garden salad, garlic soup, arroz con pollo. She left a basket of bread, and he tore into it.

He cherished appetite, how it made everything look good. The first taste was a revelation. Then satiation, then beyond— you swore you'd never eat again. But time passed, hunger rose, and once more everything looked good. A mundane miracle.

Was the charm a miracle? Or a mirage? He could take the

waitress to the bathroom and see what she had underneath her clothes. Use her cunt, her ass, her throat. Make her moan, and maybe come. But she'd forget him by the morning.

The orgiasts at the health club had forgotten him already. Had they known when he was there? Had he been there?

His meal arrived. The food was rich and familiar, and it soothed him.

What did sex bring? What was its point? Perhaps there was no point; perhaps it was all impulse. The wave of excitation over nerve fiber and muscle.

All appetite was the same. But then why did he feel closer to his restaurants than to his lovers? Something about power. Or need. If there was any difference. Was power anything except a tool to vanquish need?

"Would you like something else?"

The restaurant was closing. He knew she wouldn't hurry him, and the chocolate mousse was tempting. But she had someplace else to go.

"No thanks. I've had enough."

Oboe stumbled sleepily to greet him. David swept him off his feet, cradling him upside down. Oboe lay there placidly, four paws in the air. David carried him through the apartment, bending to nuzzle his fuzzy face. Oboe purred.

"Quite a day, Bobo." David righted the cat and placed him on the bed. Oboe padded to his corner and lay down, wrapping his tail stylishly around himself.

David took off his clothes and dumped them on the chair, then took a quick shower. From the drawer of the bedside table, he got a tube of K-Y jelly, a box of tissues, and some sheets of paper. He put everything carefully on the bed, then fetched the large envelope he'd picked up when he'd gone back to the mall, placing it with the other items. Three pillows, stacked, completed the tableau.

He lay down and propped his head on the pillows. His hand automatically found the K-Y. He flipped open the cap and squeezed a generous amount onto his palm. He gently rubbed his soft penis, lightly coating it with lube. He closed his hand around his penis. They fit well together. He picked up a piece of paper and began to read.

> *"Dearest David,*
>   *They say everything goes better with Coke. Well, everything goes better with your fingers in my ass. (Maybe you should stick a Coke can up my butt!) My hands, your tongue, the vibrator—they all feel hotter, nastier. . . ."*

He could recite the letter from memory. But the physicality of the document thrilled him even now. Iris had held this page, had made these marks.

He licked his hand to remoisten the lubricant, the K-Y tasting sweet. His penis was still soft. A hard-on was a flick away, but why? He touched himself with motions that he'd used for years.

He let himself think about the morning's time with Iris. The images bumped and crowded with others in his head. Fresh and raw, they didn't match the ones he'd polished through the months. Had Iris changed, or had the past?

He reached for the large envelope. Inside, courtesy of the mall's Pix in Sixty, were the photographs his camera crew had taken. He arranged them in a pile, then went through them one by one, using his free hand.

The first set of pictures had been taken at Gnomon Styling. Most of the salon's chairs were occupied by women who were enjoying other women between their legs. The fourth shot displayed Sukey, now on the receiving end of a licking. Her regal face was rapturous. David started to put the picture down, then looked again. The woman with her mouth on Sukey was Alice, her friend from the bookstore.

The Beneath It All set showed a shop that had become one big changing room. The customers after David had left must have taken their cue from the charmed women. Several photographs showed women bare-breasted in the bra section, and a well-timed shot had caught the shapely backside of a woman putting on or taking off a bathing suit.

One of the photographers had tracked down Lady Godiva in a jewelry store. The clerk behind the counter was placing a silver necklace on her. He wasn't looking at her neck. A wider shot showed she'd picked up an entourage of five admiring men. David hoped that she'd enjoyed the chocolate.

His hand felt friendly on his penis. Sensual, not sexual. Nice.

The wet T-shirt contest had gotten out of hand. Lots of damp, nipple-stretched fabric was on display, but two women had dispensed with shirts altogether, and a third was in the process of doing so. At the back of one picture, he could see a contestant was blatantly bribing a judge with her body.

A picture from the day spa brought him up short. Whoever had taken it knew a lot about portrait photography, and they had framed Stellina's face perfectly in close-up, every detail razor sharp. Her best friend wouldn't have recognized her. Her protein facial was complete, the eye pads barely visible beneath the semen. She must have been breathing through her mouth. The next shot was wider, and showed the boys' other targets. Stellina's hair was matted with come, and someone had ripped open her blouse and raised her bra to expose her now-spattered breasts.

David put the picture down.

Suppose his whole day had been photographed. What would the pictures show?

He closed his eyes.

"Melissa Natrova, Tired Witch. Hi, Dave."

"You got caller ID?"

"It's 11:30. All my reasonable clients are asleep. Let me guess—you want another Potency Pack."

"No, I'm calling for a favor."

"I see you've confused me with Santa Fucking Claus."

"No, I just . . . how about if I buy a favor?"

"I'm listening."

"I want one of the women to remember what we did."

"You think your pussy eating will bring Iris back?"

"No, I don't, but . . . I didn't tell you I went down on her. How'd you know?"

"There was a piece on *Oprah*."

"Try again."

"I've been watching you all day."

"Again."

"No, it's true. I saw you fuck and suck her."

"Witches can do that kind of thing?"

"My god, I've got the only client who's never seen *The Wizard of Oz*."

Questions leapt to David's mind, but time was almost gone. "No, not Iris. Not that she'd have me, anyway. But never again Iris."

"What's gotten into you?"

"My getting into her. I always thought she was a good submissive slut 'cause she did everything I said. That wasn't *us,* though, that was me, and she just went along. We weren't together; we were adjacent. I saw that in our sex today."

The witch laughed. "You put a spell on her, David. That's not a recipe for reciprocity."

"But I had sex with her for years; I know the way we were. When she was charmed today, *I couldn't tell the difference.*"

"Uh-oh."

"Yeah. She was *passive,* not submissive. Close, but . . . no, not even close."

"So you want . . ."

"Priscilla."

"The AARP candidate?"

"She fucks like a hormone-crazed teenager. But what I really like is that she's *there.* It's disorienting to have sex with another person, but I could learn to like it. I'd like to learn with her."

"Suppose she doesn't want to be with you?"

"That's my business."

"My business, too. It's me."

"What's you?"

"Priscilla. This afternoon, in this, my global corporate headquarters."

David looked at the phone. "What?"

"I pissed all over you. That ring a bell?"

"But Priscilla looks nothing like you."

"Dave, Dave, you really don't get this witch thing, do you?"

He tried to make her words make sense. It wasn't easy. "So you fucked me 'cause I told you to?"

"Nah. You think I give strange men charms that work on me?"

"Do you screw all your clients?"

"Well, I give it my best shot. But I rarely have sex with them. I couldn't stay in business if I spent my days in bed."

"So why have sex with me?"

"The way you ate out Iris got me hot. I jerked off watching that. And those mall scenes made me laugh—I never knew what you'd do next. Such a relief from all the clients who think perfect sex is fucking a dozen blonde teenagers three minutes each."

David digested this. "How was it for you?"

"It's cool you'll make it with an older woman. At 112, I'm quite the older woman."

"You liked the sex?"

"You couldn't tell?"

"Then when shall we two meet again?"

"There's the minor matter that I'll soon be forgetting this."

David shook his head in confusion. "I thought the magic didn't work on you."

"The charm does nothing. But Forgetfulness isn't a spell; it's a reweaving of the fabric of existence. *All* your acts today will disappear—there's no way to save a few."

He felt pressure in his chest. "So I'm losing you forever?"

"Whoa, lighten up. It's me who's losing you."

"Somehow that's little comfort."

"You've got my phone number, my address, my URL. Call me up and court me."

David's world whirled. "Will I ever see Priscilla again?"

"Maybe. Maybe not. But whatever form I take, it always likes its butt fucked." She paused. "You know, being with a witch is . . . complicated."

"I'll get another rider."

She laughed. "Gotta run, David. I hate to talk with strangers."

And she was gone.

NOTE

The witch in this story bears little resemblance to real witches. In particular, most witches would consider it unethical to cast spells on nonconsenting individuals. Please seek professional advice before you emulate this witch or any other fictional character.

BENDING

Greta Christina

For Ingrid

ACKNOWLEDGMENTS

First, last, and most: Ingrid.

To my friends Rebecca and Nicola, for reading the early drafts and giving me way useful feedback.

To Last Gasp, for helping me keep body and soul together while I wrote the damn thing.

And last, first, and most: Ingrid.

She loved being bent over. More than any fiddling that might precede it, more than any fumbling sex act that might follow. The moment of being bent over was like a sex act to Dallas, like foreplay and climax blended into one swooning, too-short moment. A hand on her neck, pressing gently but firmly downward, felt like a tongue on her clit; a voice in her ear, telling her calmly and reasonably to bend over and pull down her pants, felt like a cock in her cunt.

She always masturbated in that position. She sometimes masturbated by getting in that position and then doing nothing else. She would stand by the arm of her sofa, by the side of the bed, at the edge of the kitchen table; and she would bare her ass, slowly, and slowly bend herself over . . . and then she would stand there, bent over, hands on her hips or behind the small of her back, thinking. Thinking about what she looked like, thinking about what she felt like. Thinking about the feel of the air on the skin of her exposed ass. Thinking about hands on her thighs, paddles on her bottom, dicks and dildos in her asshole and her cunt. Thinking about what a dirty hungry girl she was. Thinking, until she came.

The furnishings that crowded Dallas's apartment would be a dead giveaway to anyone who knew what to look for. Sofas and armchairs with wide, firm backs and arms; tables and dressers that were all waist height; a small but varied collection of hairbrushes, vintage and modern. A padded table she had had made for her, its height easily adjustable so her head and torso could be raised or lowered as the mood required. It could pass for a sewing or card table. She called it the bending table. She tried not to use it too often, for fear of using up all the magic.

It was hard sometimes. She saw a video once where a man bent a woman over a toilet and shoved her head in it while he fucked her in the ass. She thought she would pass out. She watched the scene ten times, pale, wet between her legs, a shaking hand on the remote. She watched it ten times, and then took the video back to the rental place and never watched it again. It made her stomach hurt, the thought that this act had happened—literally, physically, factually happened—to someone who wasn't her.

She did have lovers. Many of them over the years. Dozens if you counted them all, more if you counted very carefully. More than one of these lovers had accused Dallas of being a black hole, an accusation she felt was deeply unfair, not to mention inaccurate. It wasn't that she didn't want to give anything. She simply felt that what she did have to give was sufficient. Her pain, her submission, her ass in the air presented like a jewel on a satin pillow, her willingness to do almost anything a person could do in that position . . . Dallas felt that all of this was a tremendous gift. It wasn't that she didn't want to give anything. It was that she had yet to find a lover who wanted what she had to give. She found this tremendously annoying. Hurtful, too, for sure, and frustrating at times to the point of despair, but mostly just annoying as hell.

And the accusation—"You only like to do one thing"—completely baffled her. It wasn't one thing, she argued to herself on her way home from a particularly frustrating squabble. It wasn't one thing, any more than so-called regular sex was one thing. Being bent over was a whole field of things, an entire genus, with a zillion details that could vary. Wriggling and weeping versus serene submission; being gently guided to the edge of the bed versus being shoved onto the floor; jeans and cotton panties yanked down to her knees versus a flimsy skirt slowly pulled up to reveal her sluttily un-pantied bottom . . . these were distinct sex acts, obviously and self-evidently, as different as, say, intercourse and oral sex seemed to be for the rest of the world. The portion of the world that she'd been fucking, anyway.

Certain details about her lovers didn't much matter to her. Male, female, neither or both, any of these were fine. Age, race, height, weight, occupation or lack thereof, smoking habits, voting habits, all those things that kept showing up in the personal ads; none of them made much difference to Dallas. Lately, it was beginning to make less and less difference whether she even found them attractive. It was beginning to matter only whether they were willing.

For example.

There was Daria, the photographer. Daria loved seducing people into taking things a little too far, loved getting them to sign the release and then leading them, step by gentle step, from a tasteful, soft-focus nude session into something she'd have to take to Amsterdam to get published. She loved the blush, the not-so-reluctant reluctance, the shame and relief on her subjects' faces at being exposed at last. She was good, and she got what she wanted a lot. And God knows she got good pictures out of Dallas. She got a whole book's worth of pictures out of Dallas, a book she'd have been hard-pressed to get published even in Amsterdam. But she never got the blush. She had Dallas doing things that almost made her own bad self blush, and she talked to Dallas in a low voice about how many people were going to see these pictures and know her dirty secret, and through it all Dallas just smiled, a beatific half smile like she was gazing on the face of the Holy Virgin. Daria even got out the video camera, a last resort if there ever was one, and she told Dallas about all the filthy leering perverts she was going to sell the tape to on the Internet, and Dallas just spread her asshole wider, and smiled wider. Daria did finally get the photos published, some of them anyway, and she sent Dallas five copies of the book, and Dallas sent back a very sweet thank-you note with an order for ten more copies at the 20 percent discount agreed on in their contract.

There was Jack. That was good for a while. Jack liked a lot of different things, but he was happy to oblige Dallas as long as she was happy to oblige him back. It was pretty damn fun, actually; he knew where she lived, so he could keep her on the hook for hours, groveling on the floor begging for his cock, smacking herself in the pussy and calling herself a cheap whore, bound on her back with his Jockeys in her mouth while he jerked off in her face and told her what a good girl she was. As long as he held out the promise of bending her over and doing things to her from behind, she'd do just about anything for him, and do it with a song in her heart. But he knew her heart wasn't in it. He knew that all she really wanted was the bending-over part, and someone who craved it as much as she did. And he didn't. It was perfectly fine, but he didn't have that sort of dedication to the one fetish. His fetish was variety. And ultimately, what he wanted was someone who wanted him, someone desperate for his particular cock, his Jockeys in their mouth, someone who wasn't just lending him their mouth as a trade-off for his hands on their ass. So the two of them broke it off. They were still friends, though, and they still did it sometimes, when her ads were running dry and his boyfriend had other plans.

There was B.J., a butch top who'd call herself that to anyone who would listen. She loved having cute girls bend over for her, loved to beat them until they cried prettily and begged her to stop. But Dallas never would. Oh, she'd cry all right; she'd cry and whimper, scream and wriggle, yank frantically against her ropes or beat her fists on the bed. But she never asked B.J. to stop. Not once. B.J. would beat her until the welts ran together; but when she dropped the belt and sneered, "Had enough?" Dallas would inevitably draw a breath and say, "No, sir. I can take more." Like it was a fucking gift or something. B.J. didn't think it was a fucking gift. She thought it was a challenge, or a mockery even. The last time Dallas said it, B.J. shrugged in disgust, tossed her paddle into her bag, and said, "Fine. You win." She picked up her bag and her motorcycle jacket without another word, while Dallas stayed in position, bent over with one foot on the floor and the other splayed out on the bed, looking over her shoulder with a puzzled expression. B.J. gave Dallas one last withering look and slammed out the front door—and hovered in the hallway, waiting for Dallas to run out and call after her. She stayed long enough to hear Dallas make herself come, quickly and loudly. She didn't stay long enough to hear Dallas pick up the phone and call Jack for a lengthy gripe-fest about asshole tricks who thought sex was a competition.

There was Jeffrey—Jeff, Jeffrey, he didn't care—who met her through her ad online. He couldn't believe his luck; they'd been talking in the coffee shop for maybe five minutes when she looked him up and down and said calmly, "So if I take you back to my place now, will you bend me over and fuck me in the ass?" At first he thought it was a scam, thought her boyfriend would jump out from behind her door and mug him or something; but she sighed impatiently and said, "Fine. Your place, my place. A motel. Whatever." He dropped a twenty on the coffee shop table and took her to a motel down the block. And then he really couldn't believe his luck. The door shut behind them, and she tossed her purse in the corner, jerked up her skirt, flopped over the dresser, spread her ass cheeks apart with her hands, and started begging him to stick it in. She didn't have to beg him twice. He scrambled out of his pants, shoved a condom onto his dick, and hastily guided himself into her open, gentle asshole. He fucked her slow and sweet until she squirmed and bucked and whimpered for him to fuck her hard and fast, and then he slammed her, five or six good slams before he came. But then she started getting weird on him. She stayed bent over the dresser even after he pulled out, and she started talking about him putting things into her ass. She had some things in her purse, she said. When he went silent she started sweet-talking, saying they could do it anywhere he wanted, on the floor, against the wall, in the bathroom over the toilet seat. Her voice trembled a bit when she mentioned the toilet seat. When he stayed silent, she looked abashed, said she knew she was hard to deal with sometimes, said she could see why he might be angry, said if he felt like he had to punish her she'd understand. At which point he remembered an urgent appointment, scrambled back into his pants, and made the most graceful thirty-second exit he could muster. He wasn't sure, but he thought he saw her reaching for her purse as he closed the door.

There was Betsy.

Betsy saw Dallas's ad on the Net. She liked how direct it was, blunt, stripped down to the firm core of the advertiser's need. (This was after months of ad-writing trial and error, but Betsy didn't know that at the time.) The ad read simply, "I want you to bend me over and do things to me from behind. I don't want to do anything else. If you want to do that, too, let's talk."

Betsy wanted to do that, too. They talked.

"Do you like bending over?" Betsy asked. "Or do you like being bent over? These distinctions are important." It was a weekday afternoon, and the café was empty except for a somber-looking student with a stack of physics books and the pink-haired girl behind the counter.

Dallas considered the question. "Both," she replied. "Mostly the second. But both are good."

"Over furniture? Over the knee? Hands and knees?"

"Yes," Dallas replied. Betsy waited, but Dallas seemed to think she'd answered the question, so Betsy went on. "Is there anything you particularly like having done to you once you're bent over?"

Dallas laughed and blushed, at herself and at the absurdity of the question. "Oh, one or two things. How much time have you got?"

"Give me the Cliff Notes version." Betsy smiled. "We can go over details later."

"The Cliff Notes. Well. Pain. Fucking, ass and cunt. Submission. Humiliation. Exhibition. Violation. Power and control stuff. Ummm . . . I think that's most of it. I'm sure I'm missing something—"

"Okay, I get the picture," Betsy said. "What about punishment? Did you forget punishment?"

"Well," Dallas said. "Punishment. Well, sure, punishment is fine. But you asked what I 'specially liked, and that's not really on the list. It's . . ." She grinned. "It's just a little hard to make myself buy it. No matter how much it hurts. If I'm bent over and getting done, it's kind of hard to convince myself that I'm there because I've done something wrong. But if you want to punish me, if that's something you really like, I can get into it. Do you?"

"I do," Betsy answered. "It's not, like, the only thing, but at least sometimes. So what about—is there anything you don't like having done to you once you're bent over?"

Dallas smiled. Mona Lisa with a canary in her mouth. "Not that I've found yet."

She thought for a moment and went on, a bit more human. "I mean. Of course there are things I don't like. But it . . . I know this sounds like it doesn't make sense, but I like things that I don't like. Being made to do things I don't like. The more I don't like it, sometimes, the better it is. It feels more . . ."

She trailed off, dissatisfied with her explanation. But Betsy was nodding before Dallas had finished. "Yes. What you said. It definitely feels—more."

They both drifted off into private reverie, Betsy contemplating her tea and a smudge on the table, Dallas gazing at a parking meter just outside the café window. Betsy pulled out first. "Limits?" she asked.

"The usual, I guess. No scars, no trips to the hospital. Nothing permanent. Let's see . . . no animals or kids. Nothing in public that could get us thrown in jail. I strongly prefer no shit play or Nazi stuff, but if that's crucial to you, I'll deal."

"The usual."

"Yeah. You know, the stuff most people don't like." Dallas paused. "Does that sound okay?"

Betsy nodded judiciously, trying to play it cool. "Sure. That sounds okay."

"Just okay?" Dallas asked with a flutter of her lashes, and Betsy gave up and cracked a grin. "Okay, fine," she replied. "It sounds more than okay. It sounds like I've found the Lost City of Gold. Where the hell did you come from, anyway?"

Dallas smiled, more canary than Mona Lisa this time. "Thanks."

They both paused, eyes linked, awkward. "So," Betsy said. "Yes or no? Or maybe?"

"Yes."

Betsy refrained from pumping her fist in victory. "Now, or later?"

Dallas smiled wider. "Yes."

*   *   *

So they had their idyllic interlude. All of it in soft focus, lit with an amber light at a flattering angle, with music by Burt Bacharach playing in the background.

They played teacher and student, Betsy in glasses and a dark gray dress, Dallas in navy blue knee socks and a plaid skirt, standing and pouting while Betsy scolded her for inattention and poor study habits. The first time they played, the first time Betsy instructed her to bend over and pull down her panties, Dallas felt a hard thump in her clit, and she had to think hard and remind herself about the game to keep from grinning. She bent over the makeshift desk and pulled her white panties down to her thighs, slowly, making a show of shyness and reluctance. The words "bending over and pulling down my panties" rolled through her mind like the sound of a river. She savored the words, the moment, the image of the scene that she had in her mind, while Betsy smacked her bottom with a thick wooden ruler and made her recite the multiplication tables. When Dallas made a mistake, Betsy got out the metal ruler—one stroke, hard, for each mistake she had made so far—then returned to the wooden ruler for a steady, rhythmic smacking, while Dallas sniffled and started over from the beginning. Dallas liked this game—the fifth time they played it as much as the first, although in a different way. She loved how easy it was to make it go on. All she had to do was forget what nine times eight was.

They played doctor and patient, Betsy in a white lab coat she'd picked up at a yard sale, Dallas in her most respectable street clothes. She felt so dirty doing it in her street clothes. She loved her slut gear, of course, but there was something about being bent over the exam table in a cotton-poly skirt-suit and a pair of drugstore panty hose. She could almost believe that she was a normal person, could almost feel a twinge of embarrassment at Betsy's elaborate exam techniques. She felt genuinely unnerved, almost, when Betsy inserted a cold and wet rectal thermometer, or slid in a well-lubed anal speculum and slowly cranked it open to "get a better look," or told her to undress completely from the waist down and kneel over the basin to receive an enema. She could just about feel the shame and smallness, the dignity stripped, the confidence in the doctor's professionalism gradually fading into uncertainty and a vague sense that something was wrong. And Betsy came up with the best excuses for the more excessive of her outrages. Experimental equipment, nerve and reflex testing, a serious medical condition that required radical treatment; any of these could justify storing steel probes in a jar of ice water, or pinching Dallas's thighs with a pair of forceps while making her count to a thousand by sevens, or inserting a metal egg in her vagina and swiping her clitoris from behind with a slender fiberglass rod. Betsy loved this game, and was good at it. She never stretched disbelief to the breaking point, never played doctor in spike-heeled boots or put a ball gag in the patient's mouth. She sometimes adjusted her trousers a bit too vigorously, or pulled her lab coat down tight against her nipples, but nothing that Dallas would notice with her back turned. Which, of course, it always was.

They played uncle and little girl. Betsy couldn't handle playing daddy, but she could be the uncle just fine. Sometimes she'd be a good uncle—well, comparatively good, anyway—taking Dallas over her knee for a good, simple, bare-bottomed spanking, a punishment for some childish misdeed. And sometimes she'd be a bad uncle, fondling the bare-bottomed girl after her spanking, caressing her pinkened skin, sneaking a snakey finger between her legs, telling her to be a good girl and do what Uncle said . . . and getting angry when Dallas started to cry, and spanking her some more. Spanking her harder. Punishing her for crying, and fiddling between her legs while she spanked her even more. That was a good game. They played that one a lot.

They played rapist and victim, in an alley in the middle of nowhere near where Betsy worked. They arranged a time, and Betsy got there late, late enough to get Dallas anxious and pacing, jumpy, jumping out of her skin at the sudden hand over her mouth and the knife at her throat. "Shut up, cunt," Betsy murmured, as she grabbed Dallas by the hair and wrestled her to the cement wall. "Lean against it. Bend over. Now." Dallas complied, shaking, pressing her hands to the rough wall, as Betsy yanked her skirt up and sliced open the crotch of her panties. She kicked Dallas's legs apart; Dallas stumbled, and Betsy's knife was at her throat again, the other hand groping between Dallas's legs. "Stick your ass out, cunt," Betsy snarled, and Dallas obeyed, disoriented, in a well-trained response to her lover's instructions, in terrified compliance with the knife and the rough hands. She started to cry as she felt Betsy fumble with her fly, felt Betsy's dick pressing clumsily against her pussy, felt her hole being pushed open, filled up. She felt Betsy's hips tremble between her thighs, felt the stupid anger in her voice as she let out a stream of crude, repetitive cursing. "Keep your ass stuck out, cunt, bitch, fucking cunthole, I'm sticking it in you, sticking it, fucking you, fuck you all I want, fucking bitch, cunt, fucking your cunt, spread it, spread your hole, your fucking hole, fuckhole, fuckhole, cunt . . ." Dallas kept crying, kept bending over, kept spreading her legs apart and sticking her ass out, as Betsy used her cunt and came inside her, hard, jerking. They agreed afterward that it had been a good game, but not one you could play very often. Betsy even meant it, almost.

And sometimes they just played. They played "make Dallas crawl on the floor with a buttplug in her ass and another one in her mouth." Or "tie Dallas down to the bending table and fuck her mouth with a strap-on dildo." Or "make Dallas touch her toes a hundred times and smack her on the ass each time." Or even just "bend Dallas over the bed and fuck her from behind."

It was, as they say, all good.

"So is there anything you want?" Betsy asked. They were lying sprawled in Betsy's rumpled bed, in a nest of dildos and lube bottles, piled-up pillows and dirty magazines. Dallas was idly playing with the inside of Betsy's thigh.

"You mean a specific thing we haven't done yet?" Dallas replied. "Well . . . there's this thing I saw in a video once, a scene in a bathroom, this guy bends a girl over the toilet and dunks her head into it while he—"

"Oh yes." Betsy nodded vigorously. "Yes. I've seen that video. Definitely. Anytime. But that's not exactly . . . I mean, is there anything you want? Bigger than that." She took Dallas's hand and held it on her belly. "Sometimes you seem, not unhappy, but . . . restless. Like there's something you've forgotten. Is there something you want? Other than just the next scene?"

Dallas pondered. "Maybe," she said. "Can I think about it?"

She thought about it. Thought about it all that night, and the next morning. Thought about it on the bus to work, on her coffee break, her lunch break, her second coffee break. Thought about it on the bus ride home. Thought about it the next day, and the next, and the one after that.

What did she want?

It wasn't a scene. She could think of scenes from here to Texas and back without breaking a sweat. Scenes weren't hard to think of. But Betsy was right; there was something she wanted that was bigger than a scene. Something she'd never quite gotten from a scene, not even the good ones, not even the amazing ones. Even the scenes that left her blind and gasping, also left her . . . she didn't know what. She spent the better part of an afternoon doing some tedious filing and thinking about what, exactly. Not unhappy, not dissatisfied, but . . .

Unfinished. That was it. It dawned on her on the bus ride home. She felt unfinished. Hungry still. Like she'd had a huge meal, with chicken and potatoes and two slices of pie, and was still staring at the pie thinking that a third slice might be nice. And for all her sex-positive, slut-positive, I-am-woman-watch-me-fuck attitude, she still thought her hosts would think she was greedy if she asked for that third piece of pie. And not without reason. Some of her hosts had thought she was greedy for wanting the first one.

But Betsy was different. She knew Betsy wanted her to have all the pie she wanted. She knew Betsy would happily bake her an entire pie, and feed it to her with a silver fork on bone china, and then bake her another if she was still hungry for more. And she knew Betsy would get off on it. She knew her lust was safe.

The next time she saw Betsy, she kissed her hello and said, "Yes. There is."

"I'm sorry, babyface," Betsy said. "Non-sequitur alert. What?"

"Your question," Dallas answered, rolling her eyes. "The one you asked me the last time you saw me." She settled into her seat, told the waiter that she wanted water now and a glass of the house red with dinner, folded her hands on the table, and said, "This is it. I want to do it until I'm done. I want you to bend me over and do me, until I'm ready to stop."

"Okay," Betsy said. "Sure. Why not?"

Dallas shook her head. "No. I mean it. Until I'm done. Like, done done. I mean . . . don't take this the wrong way, most of the time when we stop I'm fine, we always stop at a good place. But I could also keep going. I want you to bend me over and do me until that isn't true. I want to keep doing it until I really, really don't want to do it anymore. Can't do it anymore. I want to feel . . . like, even for just a few hours . . . like I've had enough."

"Wow," Betsy said. "Okay. Sure. Should we set aside a weekend?"

"No," Dallas said. "We should set aside a week."

Betsy looked at Dallas. "Oh," she said. "Oh. Give me a minute."

Dallas nodded and got up to use the bathroom, rinsing her face and fixing her lipstick and generally killing time. Betsy continued to scowl at the spot on the table, her chin in her hand. She was still staring when Dallas came back. Finally she spoke. "No."

Dallas's face fell. "No?"

"No. We should set aside two weeks. One won't be enough. We'll feel rushed. I want to do this right."

"What if it we're not done in two weeks?" Dallas asked. It was Friday evening, and Betsy had met her after work, their last day of work before their vacation.

"We'll quit our jobs," Betsy replied. Dallas wasn't sure if she was kidding.

*   *   *

And so they had their second interlude.

Day One:

"Starting now, all you are is your body," Betsy said as she bent Dallas over the bending table and inserted a medium-size buttplug. It was Saturday, late morning. They had woken and showered about twenty minutes earlier. "Just your body, from your waist to your knees. Your ass, and your pussy, and your thighs. You're here for me to use when I feel like it; when I don't feel like it, you're still here. You're like the vibrator in the drawer, or a porno video. Get used to it."

She laid her hand between Dallas's shoulder blades, held it there for a moment, then let go. "If you have to stretch, or eat or drink, or use the bathroom, you can get up and do it, but I want you back here as soon as you're done. If your legs and back need a break, you can lie facedown on the bed for a while, but come back to the table as soon as you can." She drew her fingers across Dallas's lips like she was sealing a Ziploc bag. "Don't ask me for permission, just do it. I'm not going to gag you, so I'll trust you to gag yourself. I don't want to hear your voice. Your voice isn't relevant. Your voice doesn't exist. Until I speak to you again." She took a cloth out of a drawer and draped it over the back of Dallas's head. "Now stay."

Betsy patted Dallas on the behind and left her there while she puttered around the apartment: watching TV, reading magazines, surfing the Web. Every now and then she'd go over to Dallas, take the buttplug out, and put things in her asshole: toys, fingers, dildos of various sizes. Casually, without much in the way of intent; no sweet slow seduction, no pounding toward the finish line. Just things in her ass, there, and then not there. For five minutes, or ten, or thirty . . . poking and prodding and swirling around, then removed and the buttplug replaced, and then Dallas would be left by herself over the bending table. Or Betsy would keep the buttplug in and put things in Dallas's cunt. Toys, fingers. She'd stick in her strap-on and hold it still, press it inside Dallas's pussy for a bit, and then remove it. None of it was at a slow pace; it generally happened slowly, but in the strictest sense it wasn't a pace at all. It wasn't really fucking. It was penetration. And then it would end, as abruptly as it started, and Betsy would be gone from the room.

As the mood struck her, Betsy would go to Dallas and do things; as the mood passed, she'd wander off. Dallas could smell her own breath under the cloth, could feel a light breeze stirring her naked skin. She could hear the TV in the other room, and Betsy laughing and popping open a soda. Then Betsy would return, and there would be more things in her pussy, or her asshole. Every half hour, or ten minutes, or hour. Dallas wasn't sure anymore. She was beginning to lose track of time. The windows were shut, the drapes pulled tight. She took a pee break and glanced at the clock in the bathroom. Betsy had taken it down.

The cloth over her head and shoulders made Dallas intensely conscious of her ass. Not that she wasn't always conscious of her ass, but having her vision gone made it easier to picture what she looked like, the cloth not just hiding her head but putting the bottom half of her body in the spotlight. Like a diamond ring in one of those boxes, the jewel framed and displayed in velvet, the ring itself buried underneath, functional but not very interesting. She couldn't help but be turned on. She was naked and bent over and her lover was in the next room planning God knows what, so getting turned on was almost inevitable. But her arousal was frustrating. Nothing was being done about it. She was beginning to get that maybe nothing would be done about it. This was about getting Betsy off: her own desire, like her voice, was irrelevant. Only her body mattered, from her belly to her knees. And when Betsy was leaving her alone, like she was doing now, like she had done for a while now, her skin tingled, impatient, hungry, sad. Her mind started drifting away from her head and down below her belly, paying meticulous attention to her ass and her pussy and her thighs, which were getting antsy and edging toward frantic in their demands for attention.

She came back to earth for a minute as her knees started demanding attention as well, and she lay facedown on the bed, the cloth draped over her head, to give herself a break. Except that it wasn't a break. Betsy came in and started fiddling with her clit from behind, spreading Dallas's thighs apart, holding her lips open with one hand while she fingered her with the other. Dallas sighed with relief and pathetic gratitude as her mind raced back into her brain and her pussy gobbled up the sensation like it was starving. The relief and gratitude didn't last. Within a minute, she was gritting her teeth and balling her hands into angry fists, as Betsy twiddled idly with her clit like she was twanging a jaw harp, steady and unchanging, too fast and hard for Dallas to ignore, too soft and slow for her to come. Dallas pressed her face into the mattress and ground her teeth so she wouldn't whimper out loud, and Betsy took Dallas's pussy lips in her fingers and spread them apart, studying her, like she was checking the turkey to see if it was done. She examined Dallas's clit for a minute or so, then left the room to watch the rest of the ball game. Dallas squeezed her eyes shut tight and her pussy tighter, clenched her anus around the buttplug, then steadied herself and walked back to the bending table. I am a vibrator in a drawer, she said to herself. I am a porno video. I don't want anything. She bent over the table and tried to make herself believe it.

She was repeating these words like a mantra when the pain started. Betsy was apparently getting bored, and instead of sticking her fingers into Dallas's pussy on her way to the kitchen, now she'd slap Dallas's ass. Or she'd stop for a few moments and beat it with a spatula, or a ruler, or something hastily grabbed out of the toy chest. No buildup, and no cooldown, just a hard stroke, or a series of hard strokes, on the way to somewhere else. Dallas had no idea what was next, or when, or if. It could be the smack of a hairbrush, wide and flat, landing again and again. Five minutes later it could be the crop, whistling out of nowhere, lashing into her thigh once and then disappearing. Half an hour later it could be the open hand. Or fingers, pinching, mean little pinches on the sorest spots. It might get mixed up with other stuff, a finger tickling her clit while a hairbrush struck her on one thigh, or a few strokes with the strap-on between blows of the belt. Or it wouldn't, it would be pure, free of distraction. There would be pain, or penetration, or fondling, and then not. Just nothing. Just an empty pussy, and a filled-up asshole, and a naked ass. Dallas began to lose track of things other than time.

When Betsy finally spoke, Dallas jumped. "Okay," Betsy said. "I think we're done with that for now. You should stand up and stretch, move around a little, before we move on." She took the cloth off of Dallas's head, and Dallas creaked up and looked around. Betsy had turned the light on. It was dusk.

That night, they watched *Star Trek* while they ate like they always did. Dallas lay on her belly on the floor and ate from a tray, the nightgown Betsy had put on her pulled up around her waist. Betsy sat on the sofa. After dinner, she had Dallas lie across her lap, and gave her a long, gentle spanking, soft tapping slaps, almost a massage, while they watched a movie on TV. She slipped a vibrator onto her lap just under Dallas's hips, and Dallas rubbed against it frantically, and came, and came, and came.

They went to bed early that night. Dallas curled up on her side to drift off, and Betsy shook her. "No," she said. "I want you to sleep on your front."

Dallas stared at her, confused. "Huh?"

"I want you to sleep on your front," Betsy repeated. "I want your ass in the air, even when you're asleep. If I wake up in the night and want a fondle or a dry hump, I'm going to want it right away." She pressed Dallas's shoulder down. "So turn over."

Dallas flipped onto her belly. The skin of her ass was still sore and tingly, her asshole was still open and tender, and she was very conscious of the feel of it as she burrowed her face into the pillow. She went to sleep almost immediately; she slept solid, dreamed a strange dream, turned onto her side in her sleep. Betsy climbed out of bed at once. She removed the cane from the closet, shook Dallas awake, and pressed her onto her belly. "You get one now," she said calmly. "If you do it again, you'll get two. A third time . . ."

Still half drowsy, Dallas felt the cane lash onto her bewildered ass, like a tree branch in a nighttime storm. She screamed politely into her pillow and didn't complain, but when it was over, she looked over her shoulder with hurt and puzzlement and something that wasn't quite tears, and Betsy relented. "Look," she explained. "I'm not mad. I'm not punishing you. I know you can't control what you do when you're asleep. I'm just . . . training you. You wanted to be bent over or facedown all the time, and I'm training your body to do that." She smiled, a lizard smile, unrelenting again. "And I'm giving myself a hard-on. It gives me a hard-on to wake up in the night and see your ass in the air, and it gives me a hard-on to beat you if it's not. So deal. This is what you wanted. If you don't want it—"

Dallas sniffled, and nodded, and burrowed her face into the pillow to get back to sleep. She woke one more time to feel Betsy sigh and get out of bed; she immediately flipped over and buried her face in the pillow. She raised her ass a few inches, screamed two muffled screams, and then nodded quietly and shivered herself to sleep.

Day Two:

Dallas slept late that morning, and Betsy was already up and dressed when she woke. "Morning, cupcake," Betsy said. "You up?" Dallas nodded sleepily. "Okay, then," Betsy said. "Let's go."

She started rummaging in Dallas's closet, pulling out an assortment of outfits and laying them out on the bed. "Let's start with this," she said, and handed Dallas the flippy black skirt, the black lace panties, and the push-up bra. Dallas dressed in a hurry, and stood still while Betsy looked her up and down. "Lovely," Betsy said. "Damn."

She led Dallas to the end of the blue sofa. "Let's start here," she said. She pressed Dallas between her shoulder blades, bending her over the sofa's wide, generously padded arm. This was one of Dallas's favorite places; it felt impetuous and slutty, and at the same time completely comfortable. She pressed against the upholstery with a sweet familiarity. Betsy took her time, pressing her down slowly with one hand while she pulled up Dallas's skirt and pulled down her panties with the other. She held Dallas there for a long moment. Then she spoke. "All right. Now straighten up and cover yourself."

Dallas flinched, startled and disappointed. What the hell, she thought. That was such a good beginning. Did I do something wrong? Where is she going with this? She hitched up her panties and let her skirt fall back down, staring at the floor with a puzzled frown. Betsy took her hand, gave a reassuring squeeze, and led her over to the kitchen table. She suddenly squeezed harder, twisted Dallas's arm behind her back, and gave her a hard shove, snapping her over the table. She jerked Dallas's skirt up and her panties down, then grabbed her other arm, pinning them both behind her back. Dallas sighed, and struggled against Betsy's grip, trying to arch her back and raise her ass in the air. Betsy dug her fingers in and pressed down harder, tightening the grip on Dallas's wrists and pressing them into the small of her back. Then she let go, suddenly. "Pull up your pants, and stand up," she said.

Dallas complied, more confused than before. She followed, bewildered, as Betsy led her back into the living room and stood her in front of the leather armchair. "Kneel in front of it," she said. "Bend over it. Pull your skirt up and your panties down, and then rest your hands on the cushion."

Dallas smiled. She was starting to get it. The moment of being bent over, the few seconds in which she moved from standing tall to lowering her head and offering her ass, those few seconds felt like the Assumption of Mary into Heaven. And they never lasted long enough. As passionate as she was about the position of being bent over, and all the things that could be done to her there, her obsession with the act of being bent over was even more overwhelming. And she had never once gotten enough of it. But now Betsy was going to give her that moment, over and over again. Dallas knelt in front of the armchair, submissive, grateful, and very slowly began to bend over into the seat. She pressed her breasts into the leather and began to pull up her skirt, sliding the hem of the silky material over her thighs and slowly up to her waist, vividly aware of how she looked. She knew that the contours of her bottom were visible through her lace panties, temptingly revealed and at the same time coyly concealed. She stretched and arched, and felt her flesh swell against the thin fabric. She hitched her thumbs into the waistband of her panties and began to slide them down, paying careful attention to every inch of skin she exposed to her lover. When she had pulled her panties all the way down to her thighs, she placed her hands on the cushion, rested her face between them, and waited peacefully.

Betsy watched her quietly for a moment, then spoke. "Okay. Get up. Let's try a costume change. The hot pants, I think."

Betsy didn't even bother pulling Dallas's hot pants down. She just bent her over the back of the faded maroon love seat, then made her stand up and do it again, watching the curve of her cheeks bulge out from the bottom of the cheap shiny fabric. She made Dallas get up and do it again, this time kneeling on the floor to bend over the coffee table. Then another costume change: she put Dallas in the plaid skirt and knee socks, and bent her over the computer table, stern and severe. Then over the ottoman, sweet and nasty. Over the blue sofa again, this time in a long full skirt and no panties, with a good five minutes to pull the skirt all the way up. Dallas was getting dizzy. The slow rhythm of being bent over and straightened up, bent over and straightened up, made her feel like she was getting fucked; but instead of each stroke lasting a few seconds, each of these strokes lasted a minute or more, and the whole thing was taking hours. She felt like she was being fucked, not in her cunt or her ass, but in her brain, and in her bones and muscles. Betsy raised the bending table up to its highest height and bent Dallas over it, her jeans and cotton panties pulled down to her ankles. She made Dallas get up, lowered the table an inch, and did it all again. Another inch, and then again. And again, until Dallas had been bent over her beloved table at every possible angle. Dallas was weak with gratitude.

When the table was at its lowest point, Betsy held Dallas over it for a long minute, letting Dallas linger on her precious magic object, letting her feel it at its most humbling angle. She then pulled her up abruptly and dressed her in a tight black ultra-short minidress, white lace panties, and black pumps. She dug a large handbag out of Dallas's closet, and started filling it with junk: lipsticks, compacts, condoms, keys to old apartments, loads and loads of loose change. She zipped it shut and handed it to Dallas.

"We're taking this show on the road," she said. "We're going to the mall. When we're there, I'm going to give you a signal, and you're going to drop this handbag and bend over to pick it up. You're going to keep your legs straight and bend at the waist, unless I tell you otherwise. You're going to do it as slowly as you can without it looking suspicious, and you're going to straighten up slowly. And you're going to do it as many times as I tell you."

Dallas's stomach dropped through her shoes. Her wobbly-kneed gratitude blew away like a candy wrapper, rapidly replaced by stubbornness and fear. She did not want to do this. She did not want to do this. As much as she loved giving it up, she was something of a control freak about it, and this felt out of control, the real and scary kind, not a roller coaster but a car wreck.

She shook her head firmly. "I don't want to," she said.

"I know," Betsy replied. "Let's go."

"Please. No. I really, really do not want to do this."

"I hear you," Betsy said. "You really do not want to do this. Now let's get going. You can take a minute if you want, but unless you're calling your safeword, let's go."

Dallas was silent on the short drive to the mall. She was alarmed to the point of passivity, and disappointed and pissed in the bargain. Just a few minutes ago she had been relaxed and high and totally sunk into her body, and now she was clenching her fingers and grinding her teeth. She looked over at Betsy, who was driving calmly if a bit too quickly, smirking at the road like it was telling her a dirty joke. It occurred to Dallas that Betsy was getting off on her discomfort, and she hunched her shoulders and glared out the window in dramatic despair.

Betsy patted her knee. "Remember our first date, honey?" she asked.

Dallas nodded, and continued to glower out the window.

"Remember that thing you said, about liking to do things you don't like?"

Dallas looked at Betsy suspiciously, and nodded again.

"So quit sulking," Betsy said. "Get into it. Submit to my all-powerful will, or something. Revel in the depths to which you will sink to satisfy my debauched whims. And do it fast. We're here."

Dallas lowered her eyes and nodded. Her irritation ebbed off a bit, leaving room for a clean, simple fear. They pulled into the parking lot, and Betsy kissed Dallas's hand. "You're on," she said.

They walked into the mall, Dallas willing herself to put one foot in front of the other, stiff and self-conscious, her gaze darting around her and then returning to Betsy's hands. They wandered for a bit, Betsy giving Dallas time to adjust and settle in, or perhaps giving her time to get even more wound up. They were in front of the shoe store when Betsy gave the signal, a discreet hand gesture, and stepped back a few feet. Dallas closed her eyes, and dropped her handbag.

She was completely conscious of her body. She knew how her calves looked in the black pumps, how her thighs looked disappearing up into the short black dress. She hung on to this anxious self-awareness, used it to remember Betsy's precise instructions and force herself into them. She kept her legs stiff, arched her back as she bent over like she was at a yoga class. She could feel her tight dress riding up. She knew that her panties were peeping out from under the hem, the curves and shadows of the bottom of her ass clearly visible through the white lace. She picked up the handbag and stood up slowly, keeping her back arched on the way back up, waiting until she was upright to pull at the hem of her dress. It was over in less than a minute.

She took a deep breath. That wasn't so bad. She was still here, still breathing. She looked around anxiously; she thought she saw a couple of guys hastily look away, but she couldn't be sure.

Betsy strolled over to her and guided her down the promenade. "That was delightful," she whispered in her ear. "A lovely beginning." She stopped in front of the record store, stepped back, and gave the signal again.

The second time was a little easier for Dallas. The third time a little easier still, and the fourth. Her body was falling into its new habit, obeying her a bit more smoothly. And it was also getting harder each time. As her body relaxed, she could feel what it was feeling more clearly, and she was increasingly conscious of where she was, and who, and why. She was exposing herself to the world, inviting complete strangers to look at her ass and see her true nature, and it was for real, not a masturbation fantasy, not a game at a sex party. It was excruciating . . . and it was why she was here, not just here in the mall, but here in the world. Each time she bent over, each time she forced herself to ignore her instincts and obey her lover, she felt a warm rush swelling high inside her belly. She dropped her purse again at Betsy's signal, and let the resistance and humiliation engulf her.

It was just getting easier for Betsy. Betsy stayed alert and self-contained, keeping her breath even and her hands in her pockets. She repeated her signal every five or ten minutes, sometimes watching Dallas as her skirt rode up over her panties, sometimes watching the shoppers as they stared at her girl. She thought that mall security might be onto them when she kept seeing the same guard over again, but when she saw the glassy look in his eyes and his gaze hovering around Dallas's midsection, she stopped worrying about it. She could see Dallas blush as she bent over in front of the pretzel stand, and felt her own pussy tighten in her jeans. She strode over to Dallas and took her by the arm.

"Now unzip your purse," Betsy commanded. "Dig around in it, fix your lipstick or something. Don't zip it again." Dallas complied, puzzled, and Betsy continued. "The next time I signal you, drop the purse. Be sure to drop it upside down, so the stuff gets scattered all over the floor. Then get on your hands and knees to pick it up. Keep your knees apart, and keep your back arched, and wiggle your hips as you crawl. And take your time. I want you on the floor for a good two minutes at least."

Dallas stared at her in dismay and disbelief. She started to speak, saw the resolve and the greed on Betsy's face, and closed her mouth. Her dismay deepened when Betsy stopped in front of the busy sports bar, stepped back several yards, and gave the signal.

Dallas took a deep breath, and upended her handbag onto the floor. She saw the keys and condoms scatter a good twenty feet away, and cringed, and dropped to her hands and knees. She tried to block out the mall, the bar, the sound of footsteps and the fountain, but blocking out the world just made her that much more conscious of herself, her body. She could feel her dress riding up as she crawled and squirmed, not just showing a tantalizing glimpse of her panties and the bottom of her butt, but slowly riding up over her hips. She desperately wanted to yank it down, to snap her legs together, to give herself some reprieve from the free show she was giving. She could feel the hem of her dress inching up over the curve of her ass, her cheeks pressing into the lace, and she knew that her ass was on display, not naked but as good as naked, in some ways better than naked. Her pussy was wet, and the panties were thin, and she was convinced that the dampness was showing through. She felt that if she pulled her dress up to her waist and her panties down to her knees, she couldn't be offering a clearer invitation. She could see the shoppers and the barflies out of the corner of her eye as she crawled, some glancing at her and then jerking their gaze away in embarrassment, some glancing away and then peeking back surreptitiously, some staring as openly as they could get away with, eyes wide open, disbelieving in their luck. She looked up at

Betsy, and saw her face, greedy, breathing hard. She could see that Betsy wasn't done yet. She deliberately knocked the condoms across the floor; she scrabbled after them, and saw Betsy shudder.

Dallas was still on her hands and knees when Betsy raced over to her and helped her up. "Let's go," Betsy said, oblivious to the furtive crowd that had gathered, or maybe just not caring what they thought. She grabbed Dallas by the elbow, hastily led her out of the mall, and drove them back to Dallas's place like a bat out of hell. She slammed the door shut behind them and shoved Dallas forward onto the hallway floor; Dallas was practiced in catching a fall by now, and she scrambled into position, knees and face on the floor, back arched, thighs spread. Betsy dropped her keys and lunged. She grabbed Dallas's pussy and began mauling her, pinching her clit, grabbing her lips in a handful and squeezing like a vise, shoving her fingers inside her sopping hole for a few quick jabs and then smearing her juices onto her lips. They both came within minutes, Dallas whimpering and licking the floor, Betsy jabbering an incoherent stream of dirty talk.

That night Dallas awoke with a jerk, thinking she'd turned over onto her side again. Startled and sleepy, she realized that she was on her belly and that Betsy was caressing her ass. "Go back to sleep if you like," Betsy said. "I'm just going to use you for a minute here." Dallas lay still, half asleep, as Betsy straddled her ass and started idly masturbating. Dallas pushed her ass up to reach her lover, but Betsy shook her head and pressed her hand into the small of Dallas's back. "Stay put," she said. Dallas was wide awake by now, but she held very still, stifling moans and keeping her squirming in check, as Betsy ground her pussy into Dallas's ass, and fingered her own clit, and made herself come.

Day Three:

Dallas slept like a rock that night, a rock with strange, intense dreams. Betsy shook her awake, much earlier than Dallas was ready for, and led her, sleepy and protesting, to the shower. "In," she said. "Elbows and knees. Face away from the faucet." Dallas complied. She was still groggy, and the blast of warm water did little to wake her up. Betsy's soapy hands on her body were soothing, the shower massager was comforting and familiar, even as Betsy directed it away from her torso and focused it between her legs. Dallas had dreamed about sex all night, dreamed that she was bending over the toilet at her office and masturbating, dreamed that her ass was being spread open by invisible hands and fucked by an invisible cock, and now she had a soapy hand on her breasts and a steady thrumming of water on her clit and her asshole. It didn't seem all that different. She noticed Betsy eyeing her watch, filed it in the things-that-will-probably-make-sense-later file, and forgot about it. She opened her legs wider to the spray of water, and came like you come in a wet dream.

Betsy handed Dallas a towel and hustled her out to the bending table, tapping her fingers as Dallas dried off and bent herself over. She pulled a chair up next to the table, and sat, and waited. Dallas waited with her, still a bit sleepy, puzzled but patient, happy to be bent over the magic table, wondering idly what was coming next.

The doorbell rang.

Dallas woke up, very suddenly, very thoroughly.

Betsy bounded to her feet and gave Dallas a reassuring pat

on the butt. "Back in a sec," she said. Dallas froze, anything but reassured, as she heard the front door open and a clatter of voices and feet pour in. "You better have coffee, Betsy," one of the voices said. "Only you would schedule a gang bang for ten A.M. on a Monday." Dallas stayed frozen, all her senses on high alert. She kept her eyes focused straight ahead, her ears tuned to the murmuring in the kitchen. She heard a familiar voice among the chatter. "Hey, pumpkin," Jack said.

Dallas relaxed. Jack was here. She'd be okay. She smiled up at him as he took her chin in his hand. "It's good to see you, pie chart," he said. "It's been ages. Sheesh, you get a good piece of tail and you disappear off the planet. You never call, you never write. . . ."

Dallas propped herself up on her elbows. "I know. I suck. How've you been? How's Bobby?" She peered over her shoulder, stealing her first anxious look at the group in the kitchen. "Is he here?"

"Nah. You know Bobby and girls. He's hopeless. If he saw a naked pussy, he'd probably die of shock. He said to say hi, though."

He stroked her hair as they chatted, and her breathing started returning to normal. He rested his hand on her shoulder as Betsy led the group in from the kitchen, and he pressed firmly as Dallas tensed up again. "Okay," Betsy said. "Everybody ready? Let's have some introductions." She quickly paraded the small group in front of Dallas's widening eyes. "Dallas, this is Roger, Ben, Lizzy, and Cheryl. Jack you already know. They're going to beat you and fuck you. Jack, you're already there, why don't you start us off?"

After that, things got a little strange.

She knew that Jack went first, knew it was his hand that moved from her shoulder and snaked down her spine and over her bottom. She knew that his second hand was joining the first, knew he was spreading her cheeks open, carefully examining her asshole, just as if he hadn't seen it a dozen times before.

And then . . . it wasn't a blur, it was much too clear for a blur, she knew every detail of what happened, but she could never remember later what came when, or in what order. Her libido was like a kid in a candy store, with a fifty-dollar bill and a free afternoon. Everywhere she turned, there was something to do, something to feel, something to pay attention to. Roger's cock was in her ass now, and if she lost interest in it even for a second, all she had to do was switch her attention, like changing channels, to Ben's hands gripping her wrists and pressing them into the table, or Cheryl's voice in her ear telling her how she was going to put Dallas's picture in the escort ads and pimp her out. Or she'd picture what she looked like, step back in her mind and watch herself get bent over and pinned down and buggered, like she was watching a dirty movie. And five minutes later, there'd be something else to do, to feel, to pay attention to. There was a blindfold over her eyes and her favorite vibrator between her legs, pulled away suddenly as a bamboo cane lashed down like lightning onto her ass; she screamed, and it all happened again, around in a circle: the sweet insistent buzzing between her legs, the quick moment of silence and stillness, the microsecond of blackout pain, the glowing after burn on her ass, joining with the return of the buzzing on her clit to make her wriggle and whimper. Then the channel changed, and she was on the floor bent over a pile of pillows, her face buried in Jack's bare feet, breathing in his familiar scent, licking between his toes like they were vulvas. She saw Betsy move behind her, and she arched her back, getting ready for a finger or a paddle or God knows what; but Betsy just stood there watching, and Dallas smiled around Jack's toes, and writhed her ass for her lover like a peep-show dancer. Then the channel changed again, and a soft, semi-erect dick slipped into Dallas's mouth—Ben's, she thought, but she wasn't sure, she couldn't see his face, and she was starting to lose track of all the new names. The owner of the dick didn't pump her or move her head; he simply inserted his dick into her mouth and held it there, filling her mouth, sealing it shut. She sucked on it like a pacifier, like a bottle of whiskey.

And five minutes later, there'd be something else. There was always something else. Her world had turned into an enormous buffet dinner, elaborately prepared and perpetually restocked, her greed satisfied within moments of her noticing it. The easy stuff, like the bootlicking and the spankings, she gobbled up like potato chips; the hard stuff, like the deep throating and the push-ups and that god-awful stinging thing of Lizzy's, she shivered over and savored like good, fiery bourbon. At the same time her brain was getting confused, irritated with the effort of assimilat-ing the input and trying to assign it meaning. She was crawling from person to person now, around in a circle again, nose to the floor, knees apart, begging each new person for some new indig-nity, saying words she had been told to say by the one before; kneeling behind Ben and begging to lick his asshole, begging Roger to ride her like a pony, spreading her asshole in front of Lizzy and begging her to whip it. They complied with her pleas, and she was exposed and humiliated; or they refused her pleas, and she was shamed and defeated. The argument in her body be-came strident, her brain saying, "Enough already, call your fucking safeword"; her libido saying, "Not enough, not nearly enough, not yet."

After some amount of time, a practical voice swam to the surface and demanded attention, and she cleared her throat and asked for a pee break. Betsy untied her at once, took the buttplug from her ass, and led her to the bathroom. "Do you just need to pee, or do you need a break?" she asked.

"Huh?" Dallas mumbled, confused, inarticulate. "I have to pee. Can I pee?"

"Good," Betsy said. She guided Dallas into the bathtub. "Hands and knees," she said. "Wait." She called out to the living room. "Hey, guys, come on in." Dallas crumpled, as the group tromped into the bathroom and stood around the tub, watching, waiting. She was tired, she wanted to stop now, she wanted to curl up in the tub and cry herself to sleep. But she could feel another layer under the tears, something that wanted to stay, something that was quiet and soft and wanted to be seen. So she arched her back, and spread her knees so they could see, and peed in the tub, humiliated and peaceful. She was an animal in a zoo, a performer in the back room of a sleazy fucked-up whorehouse, and it didn't feel like make-believe, it felt real. She finished, kept her legs open, prayed that they would go home and leave her in peace, prayed that they would pet her and soothe her, prayed that one of them would smear an evil hand over her soaked clit. She felt Betsy's hand on her shoulder, and prayed that she'd keep it there forever.

Betsy rinsed her off, gently led her out of the tub, placed her on her knees on the floor, and then bent her over the toilet with a snap. Dallas drew a sharp moaning breath as Betsy grabbed her hair and wrapped it firmly around her hand. She could feel

Betsy gesture with her other hand, could feel Jack coming up behind her, crawling between her knees, pressing his hard-on against the crack of her ass. Betsy held her there for a long minute, poised, savoring the moment. "Feel it," she murmured in Dallas's ear. "Feel it. This. Right now." Dallas shivered. She felt her knees grinding into the cold tile, her breasts shoved awkwardly against the rim of the toilet, the head of Jack's dick trembling at her asshole, Betsy's hand gripping her hair at the back of her head, her face hovering just above the toilet bowl. She was wide awake now. She held very still, seeing, feeling, listening. "Now," she heard Betsy say.

The hand on the back of her neck jerked down, pushing her head under the water, as Jack's dick pressed against her asshole and pushed its way inside. Her body fought hard against Betsy's hand, jerking and struggling, while she bucked back against Jack, arching her back, begging him with her body to fuck her harder. He took her hips in his hands and shoved into her, and Betsy yanked her head up out of the toilet and slapped her across her soaking wet face. Their eyes met. Dallas felt the joy radiating out of her face, saw it mirrored in Betsy's crazy eyes. Betsy shivered and dunked her again, and Dallas felt herself sinking into her body, her mind darting from the water in her nose to her scraped and sore knees, to the sweet, nasty stroking inside her delighted asshole, to her wet tangled hair, to the panic in her lungs, to the sudden gasp of air and the cracking of Betsy's hand across her drenched face. She could feel herself disappearing into her asshole, as Jack yanked his dick all the way out and slowly pushed it in again; then she was pulled abruptly back into her brain, as Betsy forced her head deep into the water and held it there with a shaking hand. The three of them came together,

Jack shivering as he pressed a last stroke deep inside Dallas's asshole, Dallas screaming with Betsy as she dissolved into her lover's cruel hand and her friend's throbbing cock, Betsy feeling her orgasm on the palm of her hand as she screamed and delivered the final smack.

They all held very still for a long moment, peaceful, drifting, lost in the dark. They came back to life slowly, somewhat reluctantly, at the sound of applause. They had forgotten that the others were in the room.

There was a picnic dinner on Dallas's bed that evening, all seven of them, Dallas lying naked facedown in the middle, the others sitting cross-legged around her in various stages of undress. They ate cold chicken and apples and chocolate chips, and drank seltzer or beer, and congratulated themselves and one another on a job well done. Dallas was introduced again to her new friends, and she lazily began to sort them out a bit more clearly. Roger was the slender, blond, nerdy-cute one, who had fucked her in the ass again and again. Ben was the one with the curly black hair and the crude hands; she thought his dick was the stubby, veiny one, but it had gone soft now, so she couldn't be sure. Lizzy was the brunette with the strong arm and the boots and the scary, scary toys, and Cheryl had the red hair and the gravelly voice and the really fucked-up imagination. They all smiled at her now, and petted her, and stroked her with feathers and fur, and Jack got some sort of soothing gel out of the fridge and rubbed it onto her bottom, and she drifted off into a hazy half sleep while they ate and chatted around her. She woke as they were kissing her good-bye. Jack was the last to leave. "Call me," he said. "Let's talk soon."

She nodded. "I promise," she said. She fell back asleep to the sound of her friends being politely shooed out the door. She half woke in the middle of the night. Betsy had maneuvered the blankets out from under her and had tucked her in.

Day Four:

Dallas woke at six in the morning, Betsy's sleeping hand resting on her ass. She lay awake for several minutes, holding very still. Then she removed Betsy's hand and turned over onto her side. When Betsy stirred, she shook her. "Pretzel," she said.

"Hmrph?" mumbled Betsy, still asleep.

"Pretzel," Dallas repeated. "I'm done. I've had enough. Safeword." She snuggled against Betsy's wakening body. "Mmmmm," she purred. "Thank you so much. That was . . . mmmmmm. My God." She went back to sleep almost immediately, slept for hours, dreamed of clouds and food.

Betsy lay awake, staring at the ceiling. She stared for an hour or so. She read her book for a bit. She stared at the ceiling some more. She finally got back to sleep at about nine, and dreamed that someone was throwing slippers at her window.

They both woke at about noon.

"How are you doing?" Betsy asked.

"Fine," Dallas beamed. "Amazing. Just . . . wow. Can't explain, really." She pummeled Betsy lightly on the shoulder. "So what do you want to do today? We don't have anything planned. You wanna see a matinee or something? Do some shopping? Drive to Vegas? Throw paintballs at cigarette billboards?"

"I don't know," Betsy said hazily. "I'm not really here yet. Listen . . . do you want to . . . like, talk, or something? That was pretty intense. Do you want to talk about it?"

"Not really," Dallas replied. "I know it was a lot, but I actually feel fine. Relaxed, happy, not in any immediate need of processing. Mostly in immediate need of breakfast."

"All right," Betsy said. She shrugged. "I guess you were right the first time. We didn't need two weeks after all."

"Nonsense," Dallas chirped. "It's good we had the time. It would have sucked, if we thought we had a deadline coming up. We would have felt rushed." She gave Betsy a loud, smacking kiss and bounced out of bed. "So, breakfast? Then what?"

They were waiting in line for the movie when Dallas did a double take. "Oh," she said. "God. Delayed reaction. I'm sorry. Do *you* want to talk about it?"

Betsy fiddled with her wristwatch. "That's okay," she said. "I mean, eventually, yes. But it doesn't have to be today. If you wanna see big special effects and stuff blowing up today, that's fine with me. You earned it. Ten times over."

"Aww," Dallas said. "That's sweet. But honestly, it's okay. If there's something else you'd rather do, I'm fine with that. I'm happy with pretty much anything right now."

She meant it, too. For the next several days, Dallas felt unusually calm, at peace with herself and the world. Her usual driving impatience had slipped off, and she was stopping in the middle of the sidewalk to look at trees, or sniff the fire in a nearby fireplace, or just notice that she was alive, here, in this place and time. People would smile at her as she passed, and she'd realize that she had been smiling, without knowing it, at nothing in particular. She was starting to get what those Zen idiots were talking about. She would stop in the middle of mundane events—shopping, reading, sorting laundry—and be filled with the immensity of the moment, the clear understanding that infinity and eternity were present in this minuscule sliver that was her life. Her thoughts wandered, curious and unhurried: food, dancing, illness, gardens, biology, conflict, death. Her thoughts visited these places, and were untroubled.

Except about sex.

It wasn't that her thoughts about sex were troubled. She just wasn't having many of them. Not in the usual way. She wasn't having masturbation fantasies, or fantasies that urged her to hurry off someplace where they could become masturbation fantasies. She wasn't really having fantasies of any kind. She was definitely thinking about sex at least some of the time, contemplating, philosophizing, reminiscing. She thought a lot about the last few days, and she smiled at the memories, which were lovely, salty and sweet, vastly entertaining. But the memories didn't drive her to the nearest private place to shove her hand down her pants. She would recall them happily, and then move on to the next thought.

For a bit. This was Dallas, after all. After a few days of calm, Zen-like, desire-free bliss, her clit began to wake up, stretch, shove off the blankets, and think about what it wanted to do that day. She was home alone when it started to twitch. The feeling was familiar and comforting, and with something of a sense of relief, she went over to her bed, bent over, pulled down her pants, and let her mind wander. She was a whore in an alley, bent over a garbage can with her skirt pulled up, a clumsy dick in her ass and a fifty-dollar bill in her mouth. She was in that damned mall on her hands and knees, scrabbling for her scattered belongings with her short skirt riding up over her panties. She was in a dingy basement tied to a rusty bed, spread-eagled on her back with a gag in her mouth, while a gang of fraternity boys lined up to—

She stopped. On her back? What the hell was that?

She shook her head and started again. She was in a dingy basement, bent over a rusty bed, her hands tied and a gag in her mouth, while the fraternity boys lined up. There, that was better. She moved on. She was a teenage Catholic schoolgirl bending over the Mother Superior's desk, pulling down her panties with hesitant hands. She was an exam subject in a cold white room, naked and shivering, flat on her back on a metal table—

She stopped again. Her hands jerked away from her clit like they'd been burned.

She'd had disturbing thoughts pop up in her fantasies before. Faces that she didn't want to think about that way—her boss, her mother, some of her more obnoxious exes—would occasionally slip into the stream of images that ran through her brain when she jerked off. It happened. She didn't like it, but she was used to it, and she could generally shake off the images and move on to more comforting thoughts. But this . . . This was weird. Not weird, like walking up to your house at night and suddenly finding it unfamiliar. Weird, like walking up to your house at night and suddenly finding it gone.

She started again. She was on her back—

To hell with it. Something fucked up was going on, and she didn't want to deal with it. She stood up, jerked up her pants, stalked into the living room, and flipped on the TV.

The next day she was prepared. She pulled on a leather garter belt with black lace stockings and cowboy boots and no underwear, and a short tight black dress over it all. She cranked the bending table to its lowest point, to raise her ass up as high over her head as she could. She grabbed her vibrator, and her favorite hairbrushes, and a bottle of lube, and a series of buttplugs of various sizes, and then plonked them all down within easy reach. She snapped herself over the bending table, pushed in the first buttplug, and started fantasizing.

She started with an old favorite. She was a prostitute at a party, hired as the evening's entertainment, bent over a crate on the dining room table, ready to take the crowd on one by one. The non-fantasy Dallas reached for the vibrator and shoved it between her legs. She was in no mood for teasy buildups—she wanted to come, now. The host at her fantasy party climbed up on the table and unzipped his fly . . . but then the party crowd rushed the table, they yanked the crate out from under her and flipped her onto her back, forcing her legs apart and straddling her face. . . .

Dammit, dammit, dammit. No. She gritted her teeth. Maybe if she switched fantasies—something newer, less of a chestnut. Okay. She was at the leather street fair with Betsy, bent over with her hands pressed against a wall, with a sign Betsy had draped around her neck saying FREE TO ANYONE. A tall, ropy woman came over, said hi to Betsy, and with no introduction started smacking Dallas on the ass. She spun Dallas around, then pulled out a small flogger and aimed it at Dallas's breasts. . . .

Dammit to fucking hell. Dallas jammed the vibrator hard against her clit. She squeezed her asshole tight around the buttplug, squeezed her eyes shut, and concentrated. Betsy and the tall ropy woman dragged her over to a nearby picnic table, bent her over it, and started smacking her ass. The real Dallas shoved her pelvis against the vibrator and focused grimly on the imaginary blows pounding her bottom. The tall woman suddenly grabbed Dallas by the hair and snarled in her ear. "On your back and spread your legs, slut—"

Oh, fuck it, Dallas thought. Fine. I'll just do it, this once. Whatever it is that's going on here, I'll see what it's about, and I'll get it over with.

She took a firmer grip on the vibrator and let the fantasy go where it wanted. Betsy and the tall ropy woman at the street fair hauled Dallas over to a picnic table and shoved her on her back. "Spread your legs, cunt," the tall woman snarled. "Spread them in front of all these people." The stranger pulled out a small flogger and aimed it between Dallas's legs. . . .

Dallas came, hard, crying out. Her asshole clenched in spasms, her fingers gripped the vibrator until they hurt. She shivered, and came again, her fingers slippery from her juices, her mind filled with the image of her spread thighs and her open pussy, the strange woman whipping her between her legs, the crowd of strangers looking on. She shivered, and came again.

She stopped coming after a few minutes. She took a deep breath and slid the buttplug out of her ass. Well, she thought, that was interesting. Not so bad. It's not like I died or anything. Maybe that'll be the last of it.

It wasn't the last of it.

The thoughts kept coming. She'd try to drive them off, or she'd try to distract herself, or she'd go ahead and jerk off to them. None of it made any difference. The thoughts were there. They'd tap her on the shoulder like an annoying coworker, or scream at her cheerfully like ads on TV. Whenever she masturbated. Then when she wasn't masturbating. Sexual images would drift into her head without warning, a phenomenon she was well used to by now, but now she found it distracting and disturbing. All that wonderful Zen-like bliss had dissolved, as if it had never been there, as if it had been a lie. She hadn't stepped away from the wheel at all; she was tied to it, and the wheel was on a roller coaster. She was excited and fluttered one hour, calm and curious the next, anxious and irritable the next. Until now, she had organized her entire sex life around being bent over. She had organized her life around it, period. Everything else had been built around it. But bending over was taking up less space in her mind every day, and in its place was this . . . hole. This enormous empty place where bending over used to be. And now her whole life was built around that empty place.

The thoughts kept coming. The first time she thought about tying up that cute bank teller and making him eat her pussy, she felt like crawling out of her skin. The third time she did it, she rolled her eyes and went on with her grocery shopping; the fifth time, she reached for her vibrator. Gradually, tentatively, the new fantasies were becoming less like strangers, and more like . . . not friends, but friendly acquaintances. But the very familiarity made her twitchy. It felt like it could be a trap.

When she started fantasizing about Betsy going down on her, she began to shake. She was at the movies, at a matinee, alone. She got out of her seat, hurried to the bathroom, and sat on the toilet, willing herself not to cry.

The next day, she told Betsy.

"No," Betsy said. "What? No."

Dallas's face fell. "So it's not okay."

"No," Betsy said. "It is not okay." She stood up and paced the room, agitated.

"So, you mean it's not okay with you, as in, you don't even want to try it?"

Betsy shook her head. "It's not okay with me, as in I don't want to try it. It's not okay with me that you want to try it. It's not okay with me that we're having this conversation. It is not okay with me, period, in any way. What the hell happened? What about those three days?" She blanched. "Oh, my God. Was it the three days? Did I take it too far? Did I really hurt you? Was it—"

"No," Dallas sighed. "The three days were . . . they were . . . Amazing. Mind-blowing. Really, really good." She struggled for a moment for better words, then gave up. "It was the best thing, ever."

"So what the fuck?" Betsy asked. "How does something be the best thing ever, and then you don't want it anymore?"

Dallas shut her eyes. "I didn't say anymore. I didn't say I never want to get bent over again. I just want to try some other things, too." She opened her eyes and glared. "Anyway, why do I have to explain it? Since when do I have to explain to you why I want what I want?"

"Since you want me to go along with it," Betsy snapped. "Since I became a central part of your sex life. You don't get to just pull the rug out, and then set a bomb under the fucking floor, and not give me an explanation." She sat down, and immediately stood up and started pacing again. "Remember what your ad said? How you wanted to be bent over and done from behind, and you didn't want to do anything else? What the fuck is—"

"Yes, I remember." Dallas sighed again. "Of course I remember. But I didn't say forever, did I?"

Betsy stared as if she'd been slapped. Dallas pressed her advantage. "Do you want me to promise to always want the same things, and never want anything new, for the rest of my life? Do you think that's even remotely fair? Yes, I said I wanted to be bent over and done from behind, and I said I didn't want anything else. I didn't say I'd never want anything else ever. I didn't say I wanted to be bent over my wheelchair when I'm seventy, for fuck's sake. I want some new things now, and I don't think that's bad, and I'm not going to apologize for it. I'm not—"

"Don't get so fucking superior," Betsy snorted. "Like you've grown, expanded your horizons, and I'm still stuck in my immature, narrow-minded fetish."

Dallas threw her hands in the air. "I didn't say that. I don't think that. Don't put words in my mouth. Look, I just . . . Look. I know this is upsetting to you. It's upsetting to me, too. I didn't ask for it, I didn't expect it, I don't . . . And in answer to your question, I don't know what happened. Ever since those three days, it's been different. I've been different. Those three days, it was huge, way bigger than I expected, and that's not a slam at all; it was incredible, but it was a lot. Life-changing a lot. And life-changing things, they come out weird sometimes." She paused, scowling. "I don't know. We said we wanted to bend me over and do me until I had enough, and we did. I had enough."

"Well, I didn't," Betsy snapped. "I totally didn't have enough. I had ideas lined up for at least another week. Clear, detailed, planned-out ideas. Not to mention the stuff that was lurking on the back burner. I was really bummed that you called a halt when you did. I could have easily gone on for the whole two weeks. I wanted to."

Dallas sat silently for a long moment. "Jesus," she said at last.

"I'm . . . God, I'm an idiot. That hadn't even occurred to me. I just assumed that after a couple of days, you'd mostly be doing it for my sake. I figured you'd get tired of it way before I did. I didn't—"

"What planet have you been on?" Betsy asked. "We've been doing this for, how long? Five months? What could possibly make you think I'd get tired of it? What do you think I've been doing all this time? Mercy fucks?" She clenched her hands, then carefully unclenched them. "Look. I just want to bend you over and do you from behind, and I don't want to do anything else. And I don't get why that's all of a sudden a problem."

"Okay," Dallas said. "I get it. You don't want to do this. Fine. I'll just . . . I don't know. But you obviously don't want to do this, and I'm not going to try to argue you into it."

Betsy sat down, a bit calmer now. "Look. Why don't you do this other stuff with someone else? You know that's okay with me. I don't care if you fuck other people now and then. Run an ad or something. Get it out of your system."

"Maybe," Dallas said. "I guess that's a possibility. It's just . . ."

"It's just what?"

Dallas paused, choosing her words. "I don't know that it is going to be just every now and then. I don't know if I'm going to want to be bent over three or four times a week, and then go play on my back every month or two. That may not be enough. The way I feel now . . . maybe. I don't know yet."

Betsy stared. "Christ," she said. "I have no idea what to do with that information."

"Me, neither."

They sat for a moment. "Look," Betsy said at last. "I'm tired.

You're tired. I don't think we're going to say anything else useful tonight. Let's go to bed. We'll talk more later."

They slept uneasily that night. They didn't see each other for a few days. When they did, they had the same fight again. Calmer, and with less cursing, but still the same. They met again the next day, and had the same fight yet again; calmer still, and with more "I'm sorry"s and "I know this is hard for you"s and "I really want you to be happy"s, but still the same.

Dallas called Jack that weekend.

"So how's Bobby?" Dallas asked. She set her teacup on his coffee table and plopped her feet up next to it.

"He's good," Jack said. "He's in Seattle this week. His sister just had a baby; he's helping her out." He paused for a moment. "We're talking about getting married, actually."

"Damn," Dallas said. "Who'da guessed. Well, good for you. Forsaking all others, and all that."

"Yeah, right," he snorted. "I don't think either of us is writing that one into our vows. More like 'Forsaking all others unless they're relatively sane and know not to mess with the relationship, in which case, go boff them already.' Anyway, we're just talking now. No decisions yet." He laughed. "Except for the caterers, of course. We haven't decided about kids yet, but we know we want dim sum."

Dallas groaned. "Sheesh. Californians. What will the wedding supper be? A steamed pork dumpling and a grilled snow pea?"

"You'll probably have barbecued ribs at yours," he retorted. "With pork chops on the side, and potato salad with bacon.

Speaking of which, how are you and Betsy? Are wedding bells in the stars?"

Dallas scowled at her tea. "Come on," she mumbled. "We've been together, what, five months? Anyway . . . that's kind of what I wanted to talk to you about."

"Concerned face," Jack said. "Are you guys in trouble? You seemed so happy the last time I saw you."

"The last time you saw me, you had your dick in my ass. Of course I was happy."

"My dick doesn't make you that happy, muffin-chop. You were blissed. I've never seen you like that, and I've had my dick up your ass more than once. So what happened?"

"Well . . . it isn't her," Dallas said. "Not mostly. I'm . . ." She pulled at a lock of her hair. "You know how I only like the one thing in bed? How I just like to be bent over and done?"

Jack rolled his eyes.

"Screw you," Dallas grinned. "Anyway. I told you about our little sex vacation, how Betsy and I spent three days bending me over and doing me? The gang bang you were in, when you two had me over the toilet, that was part of that."

"Good times."

"Yeah. Well. Ever since then, I've been . . . there are these fantasies. . . ." She stopped and stared at her teacup.

"Jesus," Jack said. "Spit it out. You want to get buggered by sheep? Gangbanged by the LAPD? Just tell me."

"Okay." Dallas took a deep breath. "I've been having fantasies about doing things, sexual things . . . that don't involve being bent over."

Jack raised his eyebrows, opened his mouth to speak, and closed it. He opened his mouth again, and left it hanging open.

"I know," Dallas replied. "I'm a freak of nature. But I'm serious. This is very weird for me. Ever since the three days with Betsy, I've been thinking about all these other . . . things. Being on my back. Strapping it on. I'm even thinking about topping, if you can believe it. All this shit I used to think was boring and pointless, now I can't stop thinking about it. All the fucking time. I mean, I still think about being bent over, but only now and then. Ever since those three days."

Jack nodded. "Interesting. You found the Holy Grail, and it turned out the Grail wasn't what you wanted after all."

"No," she sighed. "No, no, no, no, no! That is most emphatically not what I meant at all. It was exactly what I wanted. It was . . . It wasn't like, You got the Grail, but it turns out the Grail sucks. It was like, You got the Grail, and the Grail is amazing, but then what?"

Jack chuckled. "Have you read the scripts for *Monty Python and the Holy Grail*?" Dallas shook her head. "Very funny," he said. "I'll lend you the book sometime. Anyway, in one of the earlier drafts, the Knights find the Holy Grail, very cool, they're very happy. And then they stand around for a bit, kind of dissatisfied, wondering what to do next. And then they decide that one of them should hide the Grail, so they can all go looking for it again."

Dallas laughed. "Yeah. That. But in a way, it's just the opposite. It wasn't unsatisfying at all. It was . . . All those years of being bent over, it was never enough. Nobody else wanted it like I did, so I always just grabbed what I could get. Like not knowing where my next meal was coming from." She shrugged one shoulder. "Now I know. I can have enough of it. So I can relax. I can want other things. And I do."

"So what's the problem?" he asked. "I've known you for

what, two years? Two and a half? And you've never not wanted to want something before. Not in bed, anyway. What's the deal?"

"Well—Betsy, for one," she said. "And for two, and for three. She is seriously not okay with this. We may not survive it." She looked down at her hands. "I never got this before, but she's into the whole bending over thing even more than I was. She has been, all along. And our little vacation didn't change her mind. I think it actually made her want it more. She got the Grail, and now she's like, 'Cool, amazing, where can I get some more grails?'" She rubbed her eyes. "I feel awful. She gave me this amazing gift, and I take it and say, 'That's great, sweetie, thank you ever so much, now here's what I want tomorrow.' I suck. I can't even—"

"No," he said. "Shut up. Look, there may be things about you that suck, but trust me, wanting the kind of sex you want is not one of them." He shrugged. "You guys just want different things now."

"So what do we do about it?"

"Beats me. Look, I hate to sound harsh, but you do about what every other couple in the free world does when they have serious differences. You compromise, or you suck it up and live with it, or you break up. This isn't the movies—being honest and brave and true to your heart doesn't guarantee you a happy ending. You can make all the right choices, and things will still suck sometimes." He patted her hand, trying to be comforting; he looked at her downcast face, and abruptly changed the subject. "So, just to be clear. These fantasies you're having, they're not just things that are fun to think about when you whack off? They're things you want to do, with your actual body?"

"God," she sighed. "That's the question before the court, isn't it? If I knew that . . . Well, yeah. I guess I want to at least try them. With my actual body. If for no other reason than to find out."

He nodded. "So are you propositioning me?"

Dallas was suddenly derailed, her mind pulled from its philosophical wanderings to the here and now. "Huh?" she said. "Oh. No. I was just saying . . ." She looked at Jack, and her mind shifted over onto yet another rail, a friendly and happy and enticing rail. "But . . . well, now that you mention it—"

Jack laughed, a deep, friendly belly laugh. "You are so easy," he said. "I completely adore how easy you are. You are the least coy person I know. I have never known you to even think about saying no when you want to say yes." He put his teacup down. "Now?"

Dallas hesitated, still somewhat derailed. But she was adjusting rapidly to the new track. "Sure," she said. "Why the hell not. No gift like the present."

"Good," he said. He strolled over behind her chair, gave her shoulders a quick massage, and sneakily began to play with her breasts.

Her breasts.

Now, that was interesting. Novel. For some years now, her breasts had been pretty much out of commission, mushed up against a bed or a table for the most part, or else dangling uselessly in the air, in front of a sawhorse or some such thing. Oh, they sometimes got clamps put on them, or were fumbled with blindly for a few moments from behind. But now Jack was circling in on them, patient, relaxed, completely focused, like they held the secret to perfect happiness and he had all the time in the world to find it, and Dallas was starting to think that he might not be wrong about that. He spent long, lazy minutes cupping and massaging the curves of her breasts through the fabric of her T-shirt, and another slow minute pulling her T-shirt up to her armpits, lingering as he drew the hem across her nipples and exposed them to the air. Dallas felt her nipples stiffen. She glanced down self-consciously to see what they looked like.

Jack began playing a bit more seriously now, tracing his fingers from the outer rim of her curves to a micron away from her nipples, then back out again, like a postulant walking a labyrinth. He teased her, pleasantly, nastily, circling his fingers around her nipples as if they might explode if he touched them too soon. Dallas squirmed and slumped back in her chair; she felt awkward, self-conscious, and Jack's sadistically patient fingers were making her feel decidedly off balance. But they were also making her feel like she'd crumble into dust if he didn't touch her nipples in the next six seconds. Jack purred; he always loved making her beg for it, whether it was with her words or her body, and she was begging for it now, letting out little whimpering moans and shoving her breasts out as far as she could. He took pity and brushed his fingertip over one nipple; Dallas wailed, and ground her hips in panicked circles into the hard seat of her chair. Her mind drizzled out of her head and distilled itself into her nipples, paying frantic attention to every spiral and brush, every millimeter of pressure and movement. At the same time, she felt a sort of calm curiosity, an inner watcher taking notes for future reference. Her nipples felt like clitorises, a bit less sensitive but capable of tolerating more, which might be useful. Especially now that Jack was pinching them. He squeezed them slowly like a gradually tightening vise, and let go sharply. And again, a bit harder each time, like a rising tide. She held her breath with each pinch, fighting the pain and then relaxing and letting it in, then letting it all rush out in a huge sigh of relief when he let go.

He squeezed her nipples then, hard, and twisted them hard, and didn't let go this time. He twisted them harder, a sharp, vicious twist, digging his fingers in deep, and she screamed, and pounded her feet on the floor, and felt a spasm shake her body from her shoulders to her belly. It was over in a second. The sensation in her nipples quickly shifted from painful to annoying, and she knocked Jack's hands away, and then grabbed them and pressed the palms flat against her breasts.

"Jesus," she gasped. She wasn't sure what the hell that was. It wasn't quite an orgasm, or maybe it was. It was fading quicker than a regular orgasm, or maybe her brain was just rushing in faster than usual to process the new information. She looked up at Jack and smiled, suddenly self-conscious again. "Hello, sailor," she said.

"Hey, little lady," he replied. "How you doing?"

"Good," she said. "Weird, but good. I'd do it again." She scowled. "But now I feel all awkward. I don't know what comes next."

"Well, we can give it a minute," he said. "I'm sure you'll think of something." He went into the bathroom to pee.

"So how was it for you?" she called through the door.

"Great," he replied. "Different. It's nice to see your face when you're coming. You really get lost; it's gorgeous to look at." He laughed. "I always did think you were a better fuckbuddy than you were a lover."

Her back stiffened. She sat up rigidly and pulled her T-shirt back down over her breasts. "What do you mean?"

"Well, you know," he said. "You were a bit of a black hole when we were lovers. Not really a black hole, it's not like you didn't give anything back, but you were awfully obsessed with your little obsession. If we weren't doing your thing, you weren't really in the room. You were pretty much . . ." He came back into the living room, looked at her face, and stopped. "What?"

She was staring at him, alarmed, pissed, her arms crossed over her belly. "You think I'm a black hole?"

"No," he sighed. "I specifically said you weren't. I wouldn't have stuck it out for three months if you were. It's just, what I wanted always felt like this . . . annoyance. To you, I mean. Except when it dovetailed with what you wanted. I always felt kind of irrelevant." He looked seriously at her stricken face and sat down. "Dallas, you're not an idiot. You must know all this, right? Don't tell me this is just now occurring to you."

She glared at her hands, irritated, queasy, silent. She stayed silent for some time. "What did you want that you weren't getting?" she finally said.

"Well," he shrugged, "some actual submission might have been nice. You know, that whole 'My deepest pleasure is to serve your desire, your merest whim drives the whole of my being' thing. And . . . well, you might have thought about doing me every once in a while. I'm not always Mister Super-Tough Top Guy. I like to take it sometimes."

She stared at him as if his skin had peeled back, revealing itself to be nothing more than a clever disguise. "You like to take it?"

"Sometimes."

She kept staring. "You like to get done."

He nodded, patiently, kindly, as if he were talking to a slow five-year-old. "Yes, Dallas," he said. "I like to get done."

His tone irritated her. "Fine," she snipped. "Mister Super-Tough Top Guy. How about now."

"Now?"

"Sure. Why the hell not. Now."

The last word came out sharper than she intended—less like a suggestion, more like an order. "Yes, ma'am," he said sardonically. "At your service."

"Fine," she replied. "Into the bedroom." She snapped her fingers and pointed.

He met her eyes, dubious, concerned. "You're not kidding."

She looked meaningfully at her pointed finger, then looked back at him.

"You're certain about this?" he asked.

Now that he wasn't being an asshole, she wasn't certain at all. She kept pointing and stayed silent, afraid that if she said anything, even a short word like "yes," her voice would crack and call her a liar. She followed Jack as he shrugged and walked into the bedroom, and settled herself cross-legged on his bed, her back stiff, wondering what the hell she was going to do now. Jack stood in the middle of the room facing her calmly, smiling, waiting. "Now strip," she said. She sounded pissed. Jack stopped smiling, dropped his eyes, and slowly pulled his T-shirt over his head. He bent over to take off his shoes. "Turn around when you do that," Dallas snapped.

He stopped. They looked at each other, awkward, nervous, suddenly unfamiliar. Jack was less arrogant now; he was playing anxiously with his belt loops, and Dallas began to panic. If I want to back out of this, Dallas thought, now's the time.

They held each other's gaze. He tilted his head inquisitively, a gesture she'd seen him make a hundred times, and she let out a deep breath as she recognized him again. It was just Jack. This would be okay. She grinned at him broadly, and he grinned back, relieved. "While we're young," she said.

Jack blushed, and turned away from her. He bent over to untie his sneakers, and Dallas watched the small, compact curve of his ass swell through the fading denim. Okay, this is weird, she thought. But it doesn't suck. He stood up again, topless and barefoot, and she hopped off the bed and led him over to it.

"Now bend over," she commanded. "Bend over and pull down your pants."

It was weird as hell, saying those words herself. Hearing them come out of her own mouth. But they still had the punch. She was just on the other side of it. She could see the words land in Jack's head, could see the squirming in his belly as he fumbled with his fly, and it echoed inside her own belly. She felt a flash of jealousy as he dropped his jeans to his ankles, jealousy that quickly turned to cruelty and a desire to make him squirm even more. "Step out of them," she ordered. "I want you totally nude."

He hesitated for a second, and she slapped him on the ass. He flinched, and complied, kicking his pants away and slowly stretching out in front of her. She bit her lip. In all the times they'd played, she'd never seen him completely naked before. He had a nice body, with wiry legs and a thin, strong back. It was a pleasure to look at, and it suddenly struck her that she could have that pleasure for as long as she wanted. She didn't have to wait, didn't have to sit through fumblings and bad guesses, didn't have to hope that he'd pick up her signals. She could have anything she wanted from him, the moment she wanted it. She could have her own custom-made dirty movie, in the flesh, for her eyes and her hands and her pussy only, just by opening her mouth. She was suddenly impatient. "Spread your legs," she ordered.

His fingers twitched as he obeyed. She opened his bedside drawer and scrambled through it clumsily, scattering the rejects on the bed. She stripped down and spent a frustrating minute fiddling with the dildo harness, tripping as she stepped into it, then struggling into a pair of latex gloves. She sighed with relief and looked over at Jack. His body was relaxing, not in a good way but in a bored way; he was slumped over the bed, looking like he might start drumming his fingers any minute, and his hard-on had dropped an inch or two. Oops, she thought. She cleared her throat. "Spread them wider, and arch your back," she growled. "Show it off." She was immediately embarrassed at herself, she couldn't believe she'd resorted to such a chestnut; but he wasn't used to being on display like this, and he slipped back into shame and submission in the moment he complied. Her embarrassment slipped off into a dark corner to mutter to itself, and her impatience returned, restless and annoyed at having been kept waiting. She lubed up her finger, and slipped it in.

He sighed as she fingered him, giving something up, letting something else in, reaching toward her with his ass to beg for more. She quickly slid a second finger in, urgent, curious, in a hurry to get where she was going. She swirled the dildo at the rim of his asshole, and pushed it in.

The rhythm of her hips and the dildo's pressure on her clit was lovely, and it was frustrating, winding her up like a toy and not letting her go. Her mind scrambled, searching for a foothold, taking a step backward to look around. She saw the bedroom littered with toys and smelling of sex; she saw her beautiful naked friend bent over his bed, squirming and digging his fingers into the blankets; she saw herself, her breasts jiggling, the straps of the harness digging into her ass, her long slender cock disappearing into Jack and then reappearing like magic. The picture in her head pushed her up the ladder, tickling the clit in her brain. "Jerk yourself off," she snapped.

The command in her voice startled them both. She felt it as a strength in her shoulders and a snarl in her jaw; he felt it like a rope around his chest that made his heart soften and his dick stiffen, and he reached obediently between his legs and started stroking, propping himself up as best as he could on one elbow. His awkwardness and obedience fascinated her, made her ravenous. "Jerk off, cunt," she snarled. "Mister Super-Tough Top Guy."

An idea flashed into her brain. She kept her hips moving while she scrambled through the toys on the bed. In the jumble of leather and whatnot, she found a small, dick-shaped dildo. "Take that," she snapped, thrusting it in front of Jack's face. "Fuck yourself in the mouth with it. Jerk off with one hand, and fuck your mouth with the other. I'd do it, but I'm busy." He complied immediately, and she twisted her fingers into his hair and pulled his head back hard, eager to hurt him, eager to see the dildo pumping into his mouth. His face was flushed, contorted around the dildo; he was clearly embarrassed, and just as clearly relishing the embarrassment. His blissful greed was so familiar to her; she suddenly knew what she looked like, what Betsy and Jack and dozens of others had seen when they worked her over. It was gorgeous: artless, fragile, stubborn. It was enormous. Her eyes widened, and then twitched: it was too much; she couldn't think about it right now. She abruptly pulled the dildo out of

Jack's asshole and started smacking his ass with her lubey hand. "Squirt into your hand," she snapped. "Now." He gave himself three hard strokes and came, moaning incoherently around the dildo in his mouth. She shut her eyes and kept hitting him, hit him until her hand hurt, until he was whimpering and shaking and clawing the sheets. Sweet Jesus, she thought. What the fuck am I doing? She pulled back her hand midstroke, coming back to earth with a splattering thud. She started caressing his ass with a light, tickling touch. "Hey," she said anxiously.

He turned over and grinned up at her. His face was vague and stupid and happy, like he'd been eating chocolate and drinking cheap whiskey. "Hey," he replied.

She drew a huge sigh of relief, and he grinned wider. "So, do you have your answer?" he smirked.

She smiled back, a sardonic vampire-lizard smile. "What do you think?"

"I'm serious. I wanna know. Is this the new Dallas, or is it just a passing fad?"

She wriggled out of the harness and sat down on the bed. "No, I don't have my answer. Bits of one, maybe. It was great, though. Judges give it a nine-point-seven. If that's what you're asking."

"I wasn't," he said. "But thanks."

She shrugged uncomfortably and changed the subject. "So how was it for you?"

"Damn," he said. "Lovely. Weird." She was looking at him intently, and he coughed and averted his eyes. "You know this doesn't . . . you and I aren't . . ." He looked down, scowling, not as if he couldn't find words, but as if he knew the words and didn't want to say them.

"Oh!" Dallas rolled her eyes. "No. No, no, no. Don't worry about that. That ship sailed long ago. This is just us. Just friends." She patted his hand. "Special friends."

"Good," he sighed, and squeezed her hand. "So, friend. I have an idea."

"Uh-oh. That sounds dangerous. Famous last words."

He stuck out his tongue. "Remember how I used to smack your pussy and make you beg to be bent over?" he asked.

"Duh. Of course I remember. That's not the sort of thing a girl forgets."

"Well, now I want to play another game," he said. "Sort of like that one." He dug through the pile of toys on the bed and pulled out a slender metal ruler. "Here's how it goes. I'm going to smack your pussy, and you're going to beg for whatever pops into your head. Whatever you want most at that moment, beg me for it. You want twenty different things, beg me for all of them." He caressed the ruler and smacked it against his palm. "I should tell you now, I'm not going to promise to do all of them. I'm not even going to promise to do any of them. I just want to hear you to say them." He stopped fiddling with the ruler. "Is this okay? Do you want to play?"

She chuckled. "You should have been a shrink. Yeah, sure. I'm game."

She shoved the pile of toys to one side, flopped back on the bed, and opened her legs, grinning. She felt oddly curious; she'd certainly been on her back with her legs spread before, but she'd never wanted to be there, and she'd always flipped herself over in her mind so she could get off. Now she sprawled back luxuriously and opened her legs, savoring the anticipation, and the novelty of it. Jack pushed her knees up and apart, and she gave a startled yelp. She was used to feeling exposed; she'd had her clothes and defenses and dignity stripped and tossed aside more times than she could name. But she wasn't used to having her face exposed along with her goodies. Her face felt like an open book, a cheap trashy paperback porno with her wet pussy and throbbing clit right there on the first page. She looked up anxiously to meet Jack's eyes, but his gaze was firmly fixed between her legs.

He picked up the ruler and started tapping her between her legs, a steady rhythm like a heartbeat. Lightly, then a little less lightly. "Start talking," he said. "Start begging. I'm listening. Tell me what you want."

"I want . . ." She went silent. What the hell did she want? This was so good, so sweet, this, what he was doing right now. She guessed she should say so. "Please, sir," she mumbled. "Please keep spanking my pussy. Please spank my pussy with your ruler." She warmed to her subject as the sharp blows stayed steady on her swelling lips and exposed clit. "Please, sir, please make me spread my legs so you can hurt me, please hit my pussy, hurt it, please."

The pain on her clit was a bit harder now, and her mind darted away from it and raced around her body. She felt empty. Where did she feel empty? She licked her lips, and started begging again. "Please, sir. Please let me suck your cock. Please, sir, force it in, slap me in the face and hold my head still and shove your cock down my throat. Oh, God, please . . ." Her mind shifted. "I want your balls now, sir. I want to stick out my tongue and lap your balls like a dog, I want you to call me a cocksucking whore while you dangle them in my face and make me beg to suck them, I want you to—"

"Beg me," he snapped. "You're not begging. You're telling me. Beg me. Cunt." He smacked her pussy hard, a single sharp, cruel stroke that wiped out her words and brought tears to her eyes. He returned to the steady, painful-but-tolerable smacking.

"I'm sorry," she whimpered. "You're right, sir. Please forgive me. Please, sir." She gasped for air and groped, as her mind filled up and started leaking. "Please, sir, oh God, please straddle my face and stick your balls into my mouth, and please spread my legs and whip my pussy. Please make me lick your asshole, please pin me down and grind your asshole into my face while you spread my legs and whip me."

Her mind was crawling all over her body, groping from place to place like the hands in her gang-bang fantasies. "Please, sir, please fuck my tits, pinch them till they're raw and then shove them together, please slap my face while you shove your dick between my sore tits and fuck them. I'm begging you, take me out on the street and bend me over a garbage can and pull my pants down and stick a dildo in my ass, right on the street. Please, sir. Please do it, right in the middle of the day, please bend me over and stick a dildo in my ass so everyone can see. Please, I'm begging you, I need it, please take off your belt and beat me and make me crawl down the sidewalk with a dildo up my ass."

He turned the volume up a notch, keeping the relentless heartbeat rhythm but striking with a sharper hand. Her eyes rolled back, and she started breathing in ragged shudders. Usually when she took a beating, the pain and pleasure were separated, even if just by a tenth of a second; there was the lovely fear and trembling just before, and then the tenth of a second of pain itself, which was in fact painful and kind of sucked, and then the sweet burning high just after, all in sequence, lined up like ducks in a row. But now the pain and pleasure were immediate, super-imposed, the wires perfectly crossed, the strands not just twisted together but fused. Her words trailed off into babbling, and she went silent, slipping gently into the electrified darkness. He smacked her hard again, bringing her back with a jolt. "Keep talking," he said.

She took a deep gasp of air, and continued. "Please, sir. Please keep hitting me. Sweet Jesus, please don't stop." Her words came roaring back, a fire in an oil refinery, a souped-up race car driven by a lunatic. "Please, sir," she jabbered. "Please, I want you to take me to a sex party, one of the skanky ones with all the single straight guys pulling on their dicks, and I want you to make me be a party favor. Please make me lie on my back and spread my legs and let my pussy get fucked by every one of those guys. Except the ones who straddle my face, straddle me, and stick their cocks in my mouth and fuck my face until I can hardly breathe. Please, sir, make me be the cocksucking pussy who lets herself get used by all the guys at the party who can't get laid." She shuddered, and kept talking, Jack's ruler driving the words out of her pussy and up out of her mouth. "Please, sir, find me a girl and bend her over the bed, and shove me down on my knees be-hind her and make me lick her asshole. Please spread her cheeks for me, sir: put your fingers right up next to her asshole and spread it wide and make me lick it clean." She whimpered, and kept talking, the words pushing and bumping against one an-other, fighting to get out first. "Please, sir, please make me spread my legs and then piss on my clit, please pin me on my back and piss in my mouth, please force your cock in my mouth, pull my hair and hold my head and shove it in and make me cry, please bend me over and spread my cheeks and make me beg you to spank my asshole, please make me grovel on the floor and spread my pussy with my hands while I lick your shoes, please make me lie on my back and finger myself while you slap me, beat me, my pussy, my mouth, force me, fuck me, my asshole, spread my asshole, my clit, please. . . ."

She was babbling now, the images tumbling through her mind too fast for her words to keep up. She felt turned inside out, her asshole and pussy and breasts and mouth and clit all exposed, all beaten, all fucked, all at once. Her legs shook and spasmed as she tried to spread them wider. Her mind swirled through her body, and then circled in tightly onto her clit, where Jack's ruler was spanking her harder, as hard as she could take it, no harder, trying to make her take it for as long as she could. All she could feel now was her clit, sore, raw, hungry for comfort, hungry for more pain. "My clit," she said. "Please, sir. My clit. Please."

"What?" he asked. "Tell me. Beg me. I'm listening. What do you want?"

"Please, sir," she gasped. "Do something. Please. Stroke it, pinch it, rub it . . . something . . . please. . . ."

He dropped the ruler at once and reached between her legs. She came at the first touch of his hand, came in a spasm that jerked her belly tight and curled her up into a ball. She kept coming as he kept his hand in place, the spasms moving up into her chest, into her throat, into her face like sobbing, and out through the top of her head.

She took a deep breath, and came again. Peaceful this time, the pleasure spreading quietly through her veins and into her muscles like an IV. The Zen-like bliss she'd lived with for such a short time came back now, drifting back into her chest like it was coming home. It had a different flavor this time: looser, foamier, less like morphine, more like laughing gas. The words and pictures that had spilled out of her hung in the air, and she arched her back and let them sink into her belly and burrow into her bones. She breathed, long, deep breaths like her lungs were bursting out of metal bands, and kept coming, or doing something that was very much like coming, not shaking or stabbing her this time, just lifting her gently, a glider in the night sky.

It lasted a long time. Jack's fingers stayed on her clit, pressing, shifting, circling slowly, as she slowly drifted back to earth and settled back into her body.

She opened her eyes when she was done. Jack was smiling at her, a little wistfully, stroking her thigh. "So," he said.

"So," she replied. She had her answer. Like a Magic 8-ball: all signs point to yes. She curled up in her friend's arms, and started to cry.

JODI K

Jill Soloway

Do you just want to go straight to the dirty parts? You will find the first dirty part not for a while—on page 164; the second dirty part on page 177 and it goes on for a couple pages; and the last and probably the best and also probably the dirtiest part—the climax you've been waiting for if you even decided to read a book about a young girl involving sex appeal—would be on page 218. If you want to, you can just read those. But if you want to see the rest of my lifescape in all of its glory, then I hope you enjoy what follows, a book, by me, Jodi K. Thank you and please begin.

Chapter One

Jodi in 1980, that's me. I was born in 1966, and it's 1980, so that would make me fourteen, obviously, you know how to subtract. I don't have my period yet (which you didn't ask, but is generally what anyone asks because that's the big thing right now). First of all it's in every single book, like all teenage books, like Are You There DUH, it's me, DUH-DUH, and on and on. Every book is wildly all about it, and if they're not about it, they're about talking about talking about it, who cares, it's so stupid. I don't even care, my mom told me not to worry, and that yes, it will come. Even though my sister Maura got hers when she was only eleven and a half! Is there something gross about that or am I imagining things?

Maura has the body of the women on my dad's side. I'm not trying to let you know that I'm skinny and she's not. I'm just trying to clarify that she has a whole separate body from my lineage. Let me be exact. I was once a small-size beanpole, not totally

155

skinny; now I'm starting to get boobs. But they're not by anyone's definition BIG. For sure. I would make an effort to describe myself to you, the reader, but I ask you, what would be the
point? I am exactly what you imagine when you imagine a totally normal girl.

Whereas with Maura—some people think she's a lady. Seriously, if you glance at her, she could be an actual woman. Even
though she's a senior in high school. She is heading from a 34C
to who knows where, maybe even a D cup, and she actually
wears lady bras. I have no need for lady bras because (in case you
don't know) they have metal in them, and I can't imagine how
uncomfortable that might be. However, it is clear that Maura re-
fuses to wear anything else.

Anyway, back to what is important: not whether I have my
period, or whether Maura is like an S in her curves and I'm like
a T in my total lack of curves, or whether I should worry about
anything anyway—but that frankly, in the eyes of a million people, I'm still a girl.

But "hey," as they say, that's fine with me. I already know
that "girl vs. woman" is in your mind as you read this. You ask
yourself about the person writing this: WHAT IS SHE? and
that's fine. And we experience it, too, on a daily basis, all of us
heading face-first into our sophomore years. We are in between
everything. It's like both: we're not girls; we're also not women?
It's weird but it's my life.

By we, I mean all girls in my grade, but particularly me and
my best friend Donna. Donna is definitely my real best friend as
opposed to all the queer and not so real "best friends" of your
childhood. Donna lives right next door to me as we both happen
to live in the exact same subdivision, which is called Chantilly.

It's not the best in the whole township of Park Village, but it's second best, which is still considered very high. The best is probably Cove Farms, which is beyond insane in so many ways, including the way in which there are no farms nor coves for miles around.

Me and Donna live RIGHT NEXT DOOR to each other, which is how we met in the first place. My family moved here when I was a freshman, last year, and my sister Maura was finishing junior year, which sucks sporadically for her. Because you come to a new school in a vacuum of not being established.

And just so you know the rest of the people who are in my life (in case I refer to them) besides Maura and Donna, you have my mother Eloise who's beyond amazing, THE GREATEST! IN THE WORLD! I love her so much, I do, oh I do. She is actually a working mom, now that me and Maura are in school. Except for the summer that just passed, when she took time off for hanging out and just doing stuff, like shopping or whatever. But she's more like a friend.

In addition, she has always been beautiful in the Jewish way, which means striking in the face, while the eyes are intense. Is she sexy, though? Of course. But with a warmthness to the vibe.

Our father is Gordon. Also known to most people as Gordon Klein, DDS. Which, by the way, does not mean he's a dentist! It means he is an orthodontist and the best orthodontist in town. His office is in the city and in his office there are three sections, he calls them "bays," and it means that he can basically be charging people simultaneously in groups of three. Now all you have to do is the math to realize the earning potential.

Next question, I'm sure: Do I have braces? Just got them off. Next question.

What is Gordon Klein, DDS, like at home?

I wouldn't even know so I couldn't even tell you! If he was at home in the house much, then maybe I could tell you. Yes, I live with him. No, they are not divorced. In a way that makes us (somewhat) different. Gordon and Eloise, aka "The Parentals" as I am wont to call them time and again, are a very happy couple. And it's obvious, which is so lucky. A lot of my friends' parents scream their heads off, which would suck beyond, and mine don't, THANK GOD.

Divorce: here's the thing. When a man leaves a family it's a black mark on the entire family. It's as if now these ladies of the family are not worth anything, and they don't get to be taken care of, as a princess might, like Courtney Tausig, whose dad buys everything for everyone, whenever. She, Courtney, is the girl with the life all other girls wish for wildly.

The mom, Ms. Tausig, has the biggest diamond you have ever seen on her finger and I'm not lying. Then she gets a bracelet crusted over entirely in diamonds, then she gets earrings like every other day, and everything always has diamonds on it!

And here's my favorite thing, better than every single diamond in the whole wild world: you know how women get after they're married? Mainly, like how they look in a bathing suit? Where they'll wear a bathing suit with a skirt, and you're like, "HEY! I know you're fat under there?" Whatever the case is with her bottom half, the husband Mr. Tausig doesn't care, he looks into her eyes with the love of adornment.

Okay, as long as we are on the subject of divorce, I guess I should just say it and not be worried as to what you'll think: Donna's parents are right now going through a divorce. But I assure you that DOES NOT make Donna "less than."

Donna's father's name is Vincent and they're Italian. So this means that they are very obviously not Jewish. Her father's name is Vincent Andruzzio and he works at the Merc (aka The Mercantile Exchange). Donna's mother's name is Temma and that's it, there's only the three of them; that's why she's an only child.

On the topic of how a man looks into her eyes, here is where things get sad. When the Andruzzios were together, I never once saw Vincent look at his wife! His eyes went past her, or stayed on the mail. So it is clear that this divorce is for the best, and most of all, he is still paying for everything including their entire house, gardener, what have you. In child support and wife support, aka alimony.

My parents barely know the Andruzzios, and how that would occur when we live directly next door is bizarreness personified. I have to believe it's because Temma smokes cigarettes every second of the day and my mom hates smoking and smokers, anything smoke-related, beyond.

Did I tell you about Vincent already? His name is Vincent Andruzzio and he's Italian. And even though he's moving out of their house, I believe he's a better father than Gordon Klein, father of me, and here's why: He actually likes Donna.

He does! First of all, he has what I call "sparkle eyes," which twinkle. He's totally bald (but just on top) which I know you would think, hey, there's no way this man is handsome! But it doesn't matter, because all you see are his eyes when you look at him, which are pretty and green in a yellow way. And long eyelashes.

Am I going on and on? The sad truth is that if I was a lady I would be wanting a man similar to this Vincent. But that's crazy beyond because he's my best friend's dad and more importantly a man, probably with more hair on his body than you could shake a stick at. I'm just trying to make you know how cute he is but not in a "looks" way, more in a natural way.

And the point I am trying to make to you now (if you are even paying attention) is that the Andruzzios have made a plan. The plan is instilled from now until Donna finishes high school, and I have to believe it's so incredibly nice of them: For now, Temma and Vincent just TAKE TURNS living in the house in Chantilly so nobody has to change. No one has to live in those apartments out by the new interstate, because number one, Indian people live there, and number two, there's nothing wrong with Indian people but it's still gross.

Anyway, even if you put all the Indian people aside for a moment, I have to submit to you that what he's doing EVEN THOUGH HE IS DIVORCING THEM is not to be faulted, in fact, it is to be praised. At least he still comes there. At least he still sees his daughter. At least he still cares for her with his heart, which is more than I can say for my own father who has never went anywhere but still seems to not be here.

Chapter Two

Okay, here is my mom in a nutshell: she never stops decorating. Seriously. Today is the day after Labor Day and tomorrow is considered the start of fall. So today, she's in her "transition" mode. We have one day free and guess how she's spending it? Taking down the red, white, and blue and moving into a harvest theme. I'm not kidding! An actual harvest theme!

The way my mom looks on the outside, the way her house appears—it's all connected, I tell you. She has this shell that she wears of classical beauty. This is what they say about her: "Great face, great house, great look." But I am sure it disturbs Maura, who is trying to force the world to focus on "insides" for once. She doesn't get this obsession with "how things appear."

In the past, before Maura got giant boobs, she actually joined my mom in their pursuits: "Let's put on lipstick, let's put on sweaters, hey." But once her body grew to such proportions as to make her stand out from the other girls in her age group, and made her have to switch friends, she no longer enjoyed focusing on outward appearances.

So around the house, my mom will be chirping a let's-put-up-dried-corn tune, and Maura is lying on her bed, soured on it all. Which makes me and Donna too depressed to hang around my house, even mildly. So suddenly we're like, "Let's go to the mall!"

Park Village South Towne if you're interested.

We are buying our Le Sportsacs for the first day of school; we are finally going to be SOPHOMORES! Second years. How fun is it not to be the youngest anymore?

Chapter Three

We just got back from the mall and you'll never believe who we saw there: Todd Sternberg. Todd lives in our subdivision, but his cul-de-sac is a few roads over; you should really take your bike to get there.

Here's a story about Todd Sternberg that I'll tell you right off the bat (so you know who he is). I felt his actual penis! I'm not lying and I wish I was. But first, let me give you the history. Beforehand, barely one thing had even happened with Todd Sternberg: the time we went to the movie and Todd put his hand on my upper thigh. Not all the way up, almost by the crack, but not? And I got that chills feeling like you get when you and your friends tickle each other's backs during sleepovers?

Seriously, did you ever do that thing when you tickle the girl's back and then the sides—closer, closer, more on the sides—so you're practically on the front? And then you stop just before it gets weird? It was that feeling in the movie theater, but starting in my legs area.

Then when the movie stopped we all went our separate ways. This next part I don't even want to tell you but I will: I was made aware slowly of the feeling of general moistness in my underwear, à la a little pee, and I even thought, "Did I pee?" Of course not. And realized it was connected to his hand having been previously on the leg. If I used the word "lubrication" straight out of Sex Education classes, I'd gross you out. But I hate to admit, I think this is what was causing it.

(Does my ignorance about the above suddenly make it incredibly clear to you that I am a virgin? OF COURSE I AM. But that doesn't mean I don't have sexual feelings of my own! And I add that I hope to God on high that by the time you read this I don't care about the general embarrassment factor any longer.)

Anyway, since THEN, aka "The Lubrication Altercation," as me and Donna say, we laugh our heads off when me and

Todd pass each other in the hallways, with a "hello," or "hey" or "hey dorkface." These are the things he calls me which lets me know he thinks I'm as cute as I think he is, even though his nose is big.

"Do you want to come over and swim?" That's what he says when he calls me up.

I'm like, "Whatever." And then I call Donna and I'm like, "TODD STERNBERG JUST TOLD ME TO COME OVER AND YOU HAVE TO COME WITH ME!"

She's, of course, "No way! You have to go by yourself! He wants to make out with you and what am I going to do if I come with, just sit there in my own filth?"

And of course she was right so I put my bathing suit on underneath my clothes—

OKAY, THIS IS EXACTLY WHAT I AM TALKING ABOUT, coming up right here. I said "bathing suit," and you immediately went in your head, "bikini," right? But this is the point I am trying to make—the answer is NO! Not a bikini. I wear a Speedo tank and I just do, and that's the reality of when you're fourteen.

Okay, maybe Courtney Tausig wears her little stretchy green and yellow striped bikini, fine. It's not that I can't. I can. I'm definitely small in every possible way. If you went to buy me something you'd be like, "size two please" or even "size zero please." But that's the point; I may be a teenaged girl and everyone thinks, okay—teenaged girl, bikini, little sexpot or whatever—but that's not how I see myself!

This is where I get so mad. How I'm supposed to be wandering around innocently being sexy, but I LIKE TO WEAR

A SPEEDO TANK, PEOPLE! And I like to be able to do this without trying to entrance people into looking at me as a sex object. A Speedo tank with a racerback.

So I wear my bathing suit I just spent a gazillion years describing to you, plus my old green Lacoste, cutoffs, Tretorns no socks, and ride my bike over. The door is open so I pop in, calling "Hello?" His mom Judith is in the kitchen at the round orange table. So I go past her and I'm like, "Is Todd in the yard?"

And she says "Yes, he's in the pool."

So I go outside, and I'm like, "Hi," kick off my shoes, make a pile of everything right by the pool. And then I go, "Oh no, I forgot a towel" and he goes "MOMMM, SHE NEEDS A TOWEL!"

Next thing I know Judith has set a towel next to my pile of clothes and is instantly back at her table with her Tab.

I get in slow. He splashes little handfuls of water at me, all the while going, "Hey dork, hey dorkus, hey dork fortified," and of course I laugh because of his cute smile, at this moment I am like, HE IS SO CUUUTTTTE!

But he never looks at me when he talks. That is the craziest part! Never ever even looks at me for a second. This is my question to you. Yes, I know how a husband of many years would look past his wife, but how would a teenage boy look past a girl? Isn't that what he is supposed to be all about anyways?

But actually anyways, here's the part you want to know, and I hope it says page 164 in the actual corner of this page, because look out . . . here comes your very first dirty part.

Me and Todd are in the pool. He's this way, I'm that, like flying fish but underwater, graceful and around. It's the middle of the hot summer, like, bake. I move my Speedo strap, and the elastic of it hurts on the new red skin already. You just want to be underwater; live underwater.

Judith is in the kitchen, a lady with a straw in her Tab. There is so much light sunny quietude in the summer afternoon air that I am able to even hear the bendy in her straw. Todd dives underwater, comes at me, grabs both ankles, lets go, swims away. I look around to find out, where's Judith now?

She's gone.

Ooops, I mean she's standing above us.

Todd is holding on to the diving board with two long-muscled arms. Slight youthful hair under his arms is all I can see in the moment.

"I'm going down for a little nap. Jodi, hunny? You see your towel?"

Judith goes back into the house, closes the screen, then closes the slider. Todd's hands are on my ankles again. He pops up, flips his hair so it goes just right when it's wet, not funny. His hair has a little roll on it, up by his hairline, like George Washington from the olden days.

Staring at the way his hair rolls.

Down to his eyes, brown.

His lashes take a quick flick look at me for the first time ever, and for a mini-millisecond in its entirety, all four of our eyes are in contact.

Now he comes up close to me. CLOSE. His nose is big. He kisses me on the lips fast and dives away again.

I haven't kissed a lot of people. This kiss was about halfway between a French and a Not. It was real, it was fast, but it certainly had the openness of his mouth involved. The openness of his mouth that scared me but felt sweet all at one time.

Now I go under, swim off, loving the pool. I love the light blue blueness and the rough on the bottom. My palms go flat, hello pool floor, did you know me and Todd are two separate fish? Where did he go?

THERE! His face right in front of mine, water streaming from each nostril. His hands on exactly where my waist goes in, squeezing, then he lets go. We both pop up. If he could say "Hi" right then he would.

And now, I find myself at the edge. The edge right under what we both know is Judith's bedroom window so if she were to look out right now, she would see nothing but nothing. Just pool, I tell you, because we are directly under her. Which means we are secret, and the secretness of it causes a tiny tensing thing like a whoop-de-doo down there. Something that says, what's going to happen, with a tightness in my thing. And I am against the wall.

Just me and my butt, hard against the wall, and all I can think is please don't let the rough part make the butt of my bathing suit even worse, make it pill up. This is my favorite bathing suit.

He is against me; I'm a little trapped. His bathing suit happens to be trunks and the fabric is big and filled with air, how silly, I think. He reaches down and holds open the elastic part of his trunks, but knowing me, I'd rather not look down there. He takes my hand and reaches into down his pants. There.

Where is he looking? Doesn't he have eyes anymore? He looks at my hand, only my hand, and positions it, as if there's an exact manner he's needing and it's up to me to do it.

Now my hand is "in there" and he presses himself against the whole sandwich of us—him, his penis, my hand, me, swimming pool wall. We smash there for a moment, then a few moments more, smashing sandwich of all of us.

The smash keeps going; we all press.

Still pressing.

Smashing; then he moves away. This back-float kick thing that propels him.

I am just left there, leaning against the wall. A small snake of white, which I know to be his sperm, floats right in front of me. I get out and use the towel Judith left for me, and ride home, fast as fast can be, in my wet bathing suit, carrying my shorts, carrying my T-shirt, carrying my shoes. Stopping in front of the mailbox to put both shoes on my wet feet.

Chapter Four

Did you happen to notice something? That in the last segment, as I was trying to talk about a feeling centered on or around my vagina and I went, "down there" instead of the word "vagina"? Here's the truth—we NEVER ever use the word vagina. Do you? Do you know anyone who does, for crying out loud? It's so incredibly unfair, guys have "dick," and they just say dick-dick-dick all the live-long day, without a care in the world. But vagina is so many syllables and it sounds like the grossest thing in the world—even the way the word sounds is like something that surely smells bad. How much do I hate it? But what else are we to say?

Anyway, on to more important things, a moment of history regarding my sis Maura. As I may have mentioned earlier, she was actually verging onto popular for a half a second once. She went and became part of this group that was all about five girls all in a row who looked exactly alike. Is it a coincidence that at the same time she became a size that was unmanageable, was the same time she changed groups? Changed from this group of girls to no group of girls?

Perhaps she simply did not wish to be seen in a bathing suit, which was a majority of what this group did over their summers. It was always, "You have to go to PV with us!" PV means Puerto Vallarta. Anyway. She dropped out of the group after a gigantic fight seriously around the same time her boobs got so big. Do you think I'm crazy that I'm connecting the events?

We (me and Maura) used to share a room but now she hates me. At the same moment she started hating all of her friends, she added me in to them. Which of course I'm sure is jealousy because I'm small and she perceives herself as fat.

And the thing is, you wouldn't even think Maura was fat if she didn't wear that sweatshirt every single time. She has two red and white sweatshirts and they're both from Wisconsin, like "Badger Country" or something, and now you don't even realize she has a waist! And that her breasts are not part of her fat! And I say, "Don't you get it?" and she says, "Don't you?"

Yesterday was the third day of sophomore year and it's already way more fun than ever. Donna and I both have lockers on the second floor and there's this CHANGE floating in the air. That "What happened to you over the summer?" thing that guys are starting to emit.

Nothing happened to me—duh—I just learned how to blow-dry my hair with a round brush and got contacts, which, who cares? But I do look better.

And now when they look at me (boys, I mean) it's as if I don't have my own eyes, it's as if I have nothing but their eyes on me. And my very own eyes are closed. So how can I look back if my eyes are closed?

So this morning I go over to Donna's house to pick her up so we can walk to the end and wait for the school bus. I just let myself in like I always do and wait for her by the butcher block in the kitchen where there's usually some cake to take a crumb of, or a box of Carnation breakfast bars. Usually it's Donna's mom Temma standing by or no one at all. When Temma's in town she's having her cigarette breakfast, which is gross.

When it's Mr. Andruzzio or Vincent's turn to be home (I don't even know what I'm supposed to call him!) then it's just me alone in the kitchen with the butcher block until Donna comes down after I scream a bazillion times. Mr. Andruzzio is always in the city at this time because the markets open before five a.m. in the morning.

But this morning, even though it's at least seven forty-five, Mr. Andruzzio is in the house. He's just sitting there. At the table with nothing to distract, such as a cup of coffee, the *Trib,* what have you.

"Jodi." He says it like he's never said it before. Like he never ever even saw me before. And here's that same thing again! That same feeling! What eyes are they seeing me with? This is what I don't understand; this is the part I want to understand. WHAT ARE THEY LOOKING AT? All he said was two syllables, "Jo-di," but the feeling goes straight to my stomach, right below my stomach but above my V., or whatever. Do you get it? I see him sitting there and I can feel it in my V.

"Jodi?" He said it like it hurt him. He said it like he wanted

169

so badly to have something for his hands, any cup of anything.

"I'm sorry," I said, "I always come in here every morning but you're never here."

"I'm usually at work but the markets are closed today," he says, as if I know what markets are. "You all ready for school?"

Well, duh, I just get up at seven every morning for absolutely no reason at all, but I don't say that, I say—"Yes."

He looks straight in my eyes in that moment. Did I tell you he was bald? Like totally on top, shiny, brown beige head. Black short hair on the sides. Did he have hair once? Why does he wear a blue terry-cloth robe? Does he wear pajamas underneath it?

Clomp, clomp, Famolares down the stairs, here comes Donna.

"You ready?"

"Of course I am."

She kisses that head of his.

" 'Bye, Daddy."

I never say "Daddy" to my daddy. First of all, it's a gross word, I usually say "Dad," but mainly? I NEVER EVEN SEE HIM AND I'M NOT LYING! When he comes home he's straight to his room to read a book about Hitler.

" 'Bye, baby," Mr. Andruzzio says to Donna, and then to me, " 'Bye, Jo-di," wistful. Wistful? Am I crazy? I don't even know what wistful means!

Chapter Five

Maura wants to get her boobs cut off. Of course she doesn't say that, she just says "reduction" or "breast reduction." I didn't even know, but I just kept hearing her stomp around and my mom and her talking in these so-called "hushed tones." It's not until I walk past and hear her say "reduction" later that night that I go and sit myself on the edge of my mom's bed.

"Why won't anyone tell me what's happening with Maura?" I ask. "She's my sister and don't I even have the right to know these things?"

My mom looks at my dad who is reading his Hitler book. Okay I have to go off the side of my theme for a half second and just say this: Why did Hitler do what he did to all of those Jewish people? NO ONE KNOWS. Okay? That's the end of it! Why does a bird fly in the sky? NO ONE KNOWS. THEY JUST DO. And if my dad thinks he's going to figure out something new about it, well, let me tell you, he's wrong. HITLER WAS CRAZY. So? It happened and of course we should never forget. I mean, if that isn't the biggest DUH ever, "never forget," like we would? It's totally ingrained into us from like the time we find out we're Jewish. It's like, "Hello, you're Jewish—by the way there was this freak who hated your ancestors and he killed six billion of them."

And of course at first you wonder, "Why?" What is so bad about being Jewish that he would have to kill us instead of move away? And then you begin to think of all the bad things about Jews that you would change if you could. You go, yes, some girls are incredibly JAPPY and that would be annoying to anyone, including Hitler—and you go, yes, some of those Jewish moms want everything, that annoys as well. Yes, gefilte fish which is something we eat at holidays which is gross, yes, that's gross, but not so gross THAT YOU SHOULD HAVE TO KILL US!

Then you go, well, I better stop thinking about this so I can think about, whatever, whatever I have to do today. So you stop thinking about it.

Except my dad. I'm serious, he never stops contemplating this event, this HOLOCAUST which happened forty million years ago anyways; he's so obsessed! And every book has Hitler in the title or Reich or Reichstag or Riefenstaller and I'm like, could you maybe read anything else once in a while? And the answer is no.

So my mom looks at my dad as if for permission, and he moves his reading glasses downward and tilts his chin into his double chin and goes, "Hrmp," which I guess is permission, so she says, "Your sister is unhappy with the size of her breasts."

And I was like, "That's because she's confusing them with her fat! She wears those sweatshirts all the time so from her neck to her waist is all one thing! And it's not! There's her boobs and then there's her stomach and they ARE NOT ALL ONE THING."

My mom pulls me in bed to crawl up on her as if I'm not yet fourteen. My mom pulls me onto her when she's sad, and this story is making her sad, which I totally don't get because it's not sad at all, it's actually QUEER. BEYOND QUEER. If Maura would figure it out, she would realize that her breasts are their right normal size for the size of her body—which is not my body at all, and not my mom's body at all—but from my dad's side of the family which includes shapely beauties like Aunt Lily and

Aunt Molly. These are not small women. These are big women and they didn't ever get their boobs chopped! I know you might think this is hilarious because boob-chopping wasn't available in the olden days, but even if it was, I'm telling you, these women would not have done it.

So my mom pulls me onto her and I lay against her shoulders and face, which I love, beyond beyond. Her face has this heat surrounding all around it because she had just gotten finished with putting on her cold cream. She is so soft and greasy I want to die all over her. I literally do, I know you think I'm queer right now and frankly I don't care because this greasiness of my mom is the warmthness of everything.

It's like she takes her makeup off at the end of the night so my dad doesn't have to look at her anymore, and she's all mine again.

Chapter Six

Okay, how boring is school, I ask you? It should be fun because we're all in here, me, Donna, Courtney Tausig, Todd, JC. The Spanish teacher is the biggest dork in the world, dork beyond, his name is Mr. Grace, but we call him Mr. Erase Face, because his mustache is clear like someone erased it. I am so serious, it has no color in it, it's actually clear.

That's why I do this thing to occupy my own brain which I like to call, "Finishing Stories in My Head."

Do you ever do that?

Just finish a story?

Okay, it's like I take a story that came out one way and I make it come out another way. I don't close my eyes, I can keep them open like I'm paying complete attention, but for all intensive purposes, my eyes could be closed and I could be sound asleep, I'm that far off in dreamland galore.

And this was the one I was in:

I'm in Donna's kitchen. I walk in just like I told you I did, but when I yell upstairs Donna goes, "I HAVE TO REWASH MY HAIR BECAUSE I TOTALLY MESSED IT UP WITH THE CURLING IRON SO PLEASE WAIT LIKE TEN MINUTES—IF YOU WANT TO GO WITHOUT ME—JUST GO BUT IF YOU CAN PLEASE WAIT LIKE TEN MINUTES!"

Of course I'll wait; I can get a late pass because it's already October and I didn't get any in September so I'll be fine if I get even two in October.

So.

Mr. Andruzzio—Donna's dad—is still there just like the other day still in his blue robe, but this time he has coffee and a paper so he doesn't have to pay only attention to me with the feeling of shock that permeated our last encounter. Today he is distracted, I am second or third on his list.

"Well, Jodi," he says.

He isn't scared to say my name in one swoop anymore; it just comes out nicely.

He looks at me in my outfit, which has fall tones because it's fall but is a summer weight because it's unbelievably hot still.

"You look nice today."

He's not scared of me anymore.

"C'mere."

Just like that, in one swoop.

And so, like a robot, I go right over to him.

"Sit on my lap," he says.

And I do, also in a swoop.

He puts his hand on the back of my hair, underneath, right at where my neck connects to my hair, and he feels it, like he's never felt hair before, then responds with a gravelly "Hmm."

Now his other hand goes onto my thigh. I look at him and smile, at how silly it is to be fourteen and on a grown man's lap. He smiles his yellow-green eyes at me, crinkle, crinkle, sparkle. I can even smell him, it's like Lagerfeld or something that has butterscotch and baby powder in it. Then he touches my cheek with his nose and I can feel two hot dragon streams onto me, and he lifts his face up so his mustache is barely above my lips and his lips touch my lips and—

"KLEIN!"

It's Donna, whispering at her loudest, "KLEIN!"

Everyone is looking at me now. I am in class right now, not in a dream of dragon noses.

"May I help you, Miss Andruzzio?" Mr. Grace, our Spanish teacher is busting Donna.

Donna says, "Oh, I wasn't talking amongst myself, Mr. Grace, I was just wanting to ask Miss Klein how to conjugate 'to dance' in the 'we' tense. Seriously!"

She waves the "How to Conjugate a Million Verbs" book at him, and I burn both eyes into her.

"Great question, Miss Andruzzio. What do you say, Miss Klein?" says Erase Face, Mr. Grace. Now he and Donna are on a team against me. She is putting me on the spot in front of the whole room and I'd like to kill her or die trying.

"*Bailamos?*" I say.

"Good, Miss Klein!" Erase Face turns away from me, finally. Donna rolls her eyes and looks at me, hilarified that I was pimped so widely like that in front of one and all to see. She gives me this face like, what the fuck were you just thinking about, spazzo?

And I give her the face, like, WHO EVEN CARES?

And then she gives me a face that imitates the face that I had on in during my fantasy, which was a slack-jawed gorilla face like a million light-years from here.

"Well?" She actually hisses out loud.

And then she lip-syncs to me, "WHAT WERE YOU THINKING ABOUT?"

What would I ever say?! Can you imagine? Oh, hey Donna, I was just thinking I was in your kitchen sitting on your dad's lap so he could feel my hair, and he was seriously about to lay his mustache on me and kiss my ever-lovin' lips, you fool, how 'bout you? Ha.

"Nothing," I mouth back.

A note comes to me from her:

"WHAT IN THE WORLD WERE YOU JUST THINKING ABOUT? YOU SHOULD'VE SEEN YOUR EYES—THEY WERE CRAZY AND YOUR MOUTH WAS MOVING LIKE A DORK PERSONIFIED—NOW TELL ME WHAT YOU WERE THINKING OF OR I WILL HURT YOU RIGHT AFTER CLASS, HEAR?"

"Todd Sternberg," I wrote back. Two words. And handed it back. She looked at it and smiled.

Chapter Seven

Have you ever played Three Minutes in Heaven? That's what we did last night. We were all in the Byuns' basement. Here's the amazing thing about the Byuns, besides the fact that they're Korean of course: they are a brother and a sister ONE YEAR APART! Do you understand?

That means that Karen Byun, who is a sophomore, can invite her friends over for a Friday night activity—including me, of course (also Donna, Courtney Tausig, and this other girl I don't know who's fat)—and all the while, her brother Steve Byun, who's a junior, can also invite his friends over.

We girls all say "I'm going to Karen Byun's just to watch TV," and I'm sure the guys are like "I'm going to Steve Byun's just to watch TV," and next thing you know you have a ten-person boy-girl party without anyone's parents getting it. And there you have it!

And Mr. and Mrs. Byun are Korean, so they generally don't talk, mostly because Karen and Steve are embarrassed beyond for their general accents, whatever. So pizza comes. Once the pizzas, the Seven-Ups, Cokes, what have you are downstairs, the doors are closed for the rest of the night. The second the doors close the downstairs becomes its own universe. We all have one thing on our mind, a version of Three Minutes In Heaven. This is how we play it, and if you play differently in your part of the country please do not spaz automatically on me because this is our version so get over it.

Steve writes down on five slips of paper every girl's name: me, his sister, Courtney T., Donna, and the fat girl. Of course he doesn't write "the fat girl"—he writes her real name, and I'm so embarrassed beyond because I can't remember it right now! So I'm just going to call her Fat Girl and if you wish to spaz spasmodically that's your problem. Then the boys are the pickers—no need to freak, we change it afterward and then the girls get to be the pickers. And you have to go with whoever you get, No Matter What, except (of course) if Karen gets her brother, or if her brother gets her. Because that's gross and if you need me to explain why, then you're gross.

And of course Todd Sternberg is there. Even though he's a sophomore, it's still guys from Track. Because for some reason once they get on a team they're like "this my tribe and only my tribe," the end. Plus there's Steve of the Byun family, and Alan and Mike who are both tall and interchangeable as far as I'm concerned. WHY do they both have yellowish aviator frames? On their glasses? How dorky does that make them? What is so wrong with contacts anyway? I wear them and yes, fine, I agree with you that the constant cleaning products and the like are a hassle, but at least I have the decency to wear them.

So we're finishing up the pizza and the guys crowd together like they're one thing, and the girls crowd together like we're one thing, but when I go to throw my napkin in the wastepaper basket I walk past them and I could swear I hear Steve say to the other guys, "Fat girls love to suck dick so I'm sure she'll suck you off in there," or something or another about the fat girl!

Oh my God, I could've died right there! First of all, none of us have ever given anything resembling a BJ, and if she does that, then I'm so grossed you don't even know.

As it happens, the names are unwrapped and the first person that gets called in is The Fat Girl, wouldn't you just know it? In she goes, with Alan-Mike-whoever-the-hell-he-is. We watch the clock and some people rush to the door listening for slurping sounds, but perhaps there are none, for they back away quietly.

When they come out I search the form of her mouth for a clue as to whether it had a dick in it previously or not, but there's nothing to behold. Next thing you know I go in with Todd and the doors shut behind us.

Stillness. Black.

His hands on my sides, kissing, closed mouth. Closed eyes, now black is blacker than blacker could be. Gentle. Is Todd sad? He seems sad in the black that you can't see anything through. Not even the hoods of his sad Todd eyes are visible to me.

And now, we have the tiny creaks of light made visible through the lines between the door parts. This illuminates us in our small room, Korean coats against us. I can see that his eyes are wide open. It takes darkness such as this for him to be willing to openly look into everything he wants to look at, namely, my eyes.

Next thing I know something resembling the feel of a chicken bone poking me just above my belt, and I realize this is his HARD-ON! Like it's trying to tell my waist something. His hands are holding on gently to my waist but his actual dick has more to say! How sad and funny at the same time!

Now there's yelling; we know time is up.

And then we came out, wiping our lips with a smile. And then a name is called and wouldn't you know it, Todd gets picked again but this time he gets Fatitude McGee, fat girl, and how much you want to make a million-dollar bet she will touch his thing. I would give anything to be a Korean coat so I could watch her. However I would prefer to be an invisible Korean coat because if they caught me watching, I'd die automatically.

That fat girl's name was Steff, I just remembered, and she's not so fat, she's just medium fat. À la I'm thin, my sis is bigger, Steff is somewhat bigger, but no one is anyone near as fat as the mom on *Good Times* or anything.

And outside the closet, while we each have one eye on the TV, on Joannie loving Chachi or whatever, and one eye on the door, and Donna wants to know, "Why does everyone keep getting Steff?"

And I'm like, "Luck," but I know it's because when she's in there she kisses their dicks. And a part of me knows that Steve knows exactly who he's picking and I was picked to prime his dick and she was picked to enjoy it.

Is that the saddest story you ever heard? And I'm sure you have just one more question if you have been reading this faithfully. Did I close my eyes when I was with Todd, you wonder, and imagine that he was Vincent and that's who I was ACTU-ALLY WITH?

That would be so obvious, but no, it didn't happen that way. Because I would never do that. Kissing Vincent is not kissing Todd and I will never confuse the two. So please don't you confuse them.

Chapter Eight

One day when Vincent had been not around for way too long I said, sincerely, but in an offhanded way to Donna, "When's your dad coming back?"

"Any day now," she said.

That was December 2 and any day now still hasn't come.

December 2

December 2

December 2

It is the morning of December 2 and it goes like this. I wish I could write a poem about it, so that you as my reader could get everything, so you could get the flowery flowery flowers and the waves that are beneath all of this. Will you come with me to this part of my tale? This is the beginning of the part that I seriously wanted you to know about.

Gordon Klein, DDS, aka my dad, left at seven a.m., riding his Buick to the train parking lot called "Kiss 'n' Ride" which is absurd beyond cuz what if you're in a fight and you don't feel like kissing? He has to be to the city by eight.

Now it's me and Maura and my mom and I'm sick with a flu. And Maura's like, "I'M SICK TOO THEN." But my mom knows it's a serious lie and sends Maura to school, packing.

Eight a.m. Door slam. Everyone leaves. Mom and Maura calling "'BYYYYYYEE"; I'm upstairs alone in my room, me and my flu. I am to take my temperature and if it goes above anything then to call.

Yes sir, the door slams. Slam it. Slam it. Slam it. Just once, but I hear it three times like a moment in a movie repeated, because it marks my aloneness. Have you ever been alone in a house and it makes you feel sexy?

In my room.

T-shirt only, underwear.

Walk downstairs. Now that everyone's gone I feel fine. Flu, flu, where did you go? I have no idea.

Carpet on the stairs.

Carpet under toes.

No one is here so I can go and lay on the couch and put on *Price Is Right* and put the bolster between my legs and just squeeze. In case you're wondering this isn't "masturbating," I don't put anything in me; I'm not gross.

The bolster is this part of the couch, like a cushion, but if you want you can put it between your legs and just squeeze while you're watching TV.

So I put the TV on, and I look at the bolster. But before I can even bring the bolster and my feeling of being alone into one thing, I hear a noise.

CLUNK. KACHUNK.

It's the garage door.

Going up.

Next door.

I run run dash dash spasmodically upstairs to my mom's room which looks out over the cul-de-sac.

Look out the window.

He's back.

HE'S BACK, I TELL YOU.

Vincent A., little does he know I'm watching him. I can't see him, just his figure in the garage. He opens the trunk of his car, removes one hanging bag, one suitcase, another suitcase. Everything now goes onto the ground to wait in a small group of luggage.

Shuts trunk.

As he turns to come out of the garage to go around the car, does he look up here at me? See me? I don't think so but to be perfectly, completely honest, frankly, I truly don't know.

And now I stand behind my mom's curtains. The curtains

are green and brown, the same fabric as the bedspread; they are lined with white cotton so I line myself with white cotton as well.

CHUNK.

The garage door closes, and as it shuts away my view of him, I run at top speed back down the stairs. Where is that flu? you may be asking right now. I would be asking myself the same question.

Into the yard, I am racing now, but low, low enough that I can't be seen. I crouch behind the chaise lounge. I am outside here, waiting for him.

I can hear into their backyard.

I can hear the slider open.

Now the screen door.

CLICK. CLICKIT.

Click and fasten, open close open close open close. The screen door is slid shut now. Or is it? Where is he?

I can only see him if I am up high.

Up high in our yard is only from the diving board.

I go to the diving board.

The pool is empty.

Why would I be on the diving board in December, on December 2, in nothing but a tee? I step up so quickly on it and see his head, looking, but not at me. He is smoking, but outside, not like Temma, who is gross.

He is an outdoor occasional smoker. Temma is a grody indoor smoker. Temma smokes herself into a smoke stew, a smell of old wet chocolate ash stew. His smoke is clean and grassy green, it helps him be part of the wind, helps his aftershave kiss him.

Hello.

He looks at me.

What am I doing standing on the diving board?

No one knows.

I pop down and run back into the house.

I'm fourteen so I am allowed to be fast and furious, missing in action.

I close the slider too. God in heaven, it is really cold outside. I'm back in. What in the world would I be doing outside with a cold or a flu?

Now what do I do?

I go to the couch and lay down. The TV is still on but now it's not *Price Is Right* anymore, it's *Match Game*.

The bolster looks at me. "Should I come and get between your legs?" it asks.

CLARP.

That is the sound of Vincent doing something, anything heavy in his house. Maybe something in his garage, moving a trash can. But to me it sounds like a bird call, or some sort of symbol that tells me to please please come over right now.

And I'm thinking, Vincent Andruzzio, I heard your CLARP and I'm on my way. See, I perfectly understand that you can't tell me to come over because you must be at least forty and that would be incredibly illegal, including gross beyond, so you make that CLARP sound so I'll know.

I know.

I sit up.

I look at the bolster.

I lay back down.

Oh, Vincent, Vincent, Vincent . . . don't you even know? I

want so badly to clamp around that bolster and have you watching me from the corner of the room. Can you see me from your house? Can you see through my walls?

The phone rings.

It's HIM, I know it's him, I know it is. I wait wait—don't look desperate—ring once, twice, ring again for good luck, ring once more for double invisible good luck. Finally, softly, not crazy with a burning love that sets me afire, I answer the phone.

(Almost in a whisper.)

"Heh-llo."

"Why'd you take so long to answer the phone?"

It's my mom. Ugh beyond. Ugh ugh ugh.

"I was in the bathroom," I answer.

"How are you feeling?"

"Fine," I answer.

"Oh, I'm so glad, sweetie."

We both pause.

"Are you sure," she asks. "You sound kinda low."

"I'm fine," I answer, and it goes back and forth like this and all the while Vincent is moving through his house. I have lost him, I don't know what he's wearing. Is he in his kitchen, his family room? I need to join him using my imagination and my brain as a tour guide to follow him around the halls of his house, but my mom is still talking and Vincent is tiny, moving through the rooms of my body and if I don't get off the phone soon I won't be able to watch him anymore.

"I have to go, I mean, I'm fine, I wanna go, I'm watching something."

She lets me go.

I hang up the phone, my finger pressing down on the clear

plastic nub. JODI? I'm asking myself. Don't hang up that phone, I'm telling myself. Release the plastic nub, let it go, and dial Donna Andruzzio's number, this is so easy, just dial it—

555-5017.

That was easy.

Ring, ring, double good luck, ring, wait—

"Heh-loh?"

Him, his voice, gravel in its very Italian-ness, no accent, re-ally, just a feeling that it is deep and coming from somewhere hard like where salami and wine come from. Far away and spicy. Red wine.

"Oh, hi" (I am surprised, I am such a good actress for my age, frankly, if you don't mind me saying). "Hi, Mr. Andruzzio, it's me" (pausing), "Jodi," I say, then, "Jodi Klein—from next door."

And I won't say, "It's me, Donna's friend," just in case. Just in case at this moment he would rather see me as a young lady from anywhere in his worldscape, not related in some way to his daughter.

"Jodi," he says, happy to hear my voice, purposeful like in my daydream, not at all awkward. So happy to hear my voice is he, I tell you.

Now I wait. I wait because this is the moment.

This is the moment he can say it: Hey, why don't you come over here, Jodi, and crawl up upon me in a sexy manner for a moment or two while I read the day's paper and tickle your hair? While everyone else is gone. Just you and me and the table and my hand and your hair. But no, he says nothing, instead, he says silence. Looks like I have to say something. I guess I should say something.

"Is Donna there?" I ask.

"No, Jodi, she doesn't get home from school until three-fifteen and it's only eleven." He says it with a lilting upward tilting in his voice, like is he accusing me of something. Of knowing better? Does he know I made this phone call so I could hear his voice from a red wine section of another country?

"Why are you home?" he asks.

"I'm sick," I say.

"Poor thing," he says.

"Oh my God. I can't believe I forgot to even look at the clock first, duh, I'm so stupid," I say.

Acting comes as naturally to me as could be. I am just becoming a stupider version of me, a version stupid enough that wants him to know how incredibly dumb I am. Dumb because my voice is high and if he wants something from me all he has to do is tell me.

Is any of this making sense? I feel that the higher my voice goes the more he will understand that his wanting of me is returned, or my willingness to go along with his wanting of me, if you get my drift.

"That's okay," is his answer to how stupid I am.

"I, um," is what I say.

"I can tell her to call you when she gets home."

"Yeah. Tell her to call me when she gets home," I say.

And then I hang up with a click and that is the end of this chapter.

Chapter Nine

Merry Christmas.

This might be the part where you want to know why we celebrate Christmas if we're so incredibly Jewish. Good question.

We just do. We do it in a Jewish way, which means white Christmas tree, blue lights. Believe it or not that makes it all Jewish. Plus my mom loves the scentedness of the wreaths, the rings of wood and holly that go on the door. She thinks if she leaves out the red then it's maybe not about Jesus and the blood that came out of him flowing anymore.

Can you believe it? I surely cannot and Maura can't as well, but we just go on and who's going to say no to more presents anyway? And my dad doesn't even say, "Jesus Christ, Eloise, we're Jews," like he used to when we were in our early younger childhood. We just try make it festive like a holiday season is meant to be, meaning, hey, we don't go to church, but more like, hey, we pay tribute to the various Americanizations of Christmas.

Chapter Ten

Last night me and Donna and Todd and Alan went to the mall to see *Blue Lagoon*. We had to sneak in. We had to buy tickets for another movie, some kids' "rated G" (WHAT AN IDIOT IS THE GUY WHO WORKS AT THE THEATER? WHAT IN THE WORLD WOULD FOUR TEENAGERS BE DOING GOING TO A DUMB RATED-G DISNEY

MOVIE ANYWAYS?) and then after the movie started, we sneak out and run to the "rated R." So we missed the first twenty minutes, but who even cares because Brooke Shields is so beautiful I want to kill myself. And Christopher Atkins is dream dream dream galore.

Can you imagine being naked on an island with Christopher Atkins? His hair is curled into golden locks, his legs are tanned with a light dusting of whatever sand has gotten on him. The sexy part of this movie is the way in which they discover how the tinglings of nature arise when confronted with one another's personhood. Her hair is so long it covers her breasts, but you just know they are under there. Their hands are tanned and hold on to each other's sides, gently, like me and Todd in the closet. Except there are no Korean coats, there are no dorks galore waiting outside the closet.

But there, on that tropical paradise of land, there are palm trees, swaying blue waters of ocean, perhaps a monkey off eeking in the distance. There are no parents around to say "yes" to this or "no" to that, just the secret souls of two young people who find they cannot live without each other.

The sexiness: great. The actual sex part: not so great. It's like something he does to her accidentally, like farting on her. If he could have said "oops" he would have. They are both so confused by it. I don't care if you live on an island or not, you know what sex is when you see it.

Afterward, we're by the fountain in the mall and Donna and Zit-face Extraordinaire are talking about Duh, how they'd never actually be able to survive on that island if it was reality and I'm thinking, It's not reality you stupid dork-ass, it's a movie, it's spelled M-O-V-I-E cuz it's a movie so get over it. But I don't say anything cuz Todd and I are at the fountain and WITHOUT EVEN LOOKING AT ME—and I am not lying here— perhaps he is looking beyond me, perhaps to a spot of neon on the window at the Mrs. Fields' Cookies, he goes, "So, do you wanna go out?"

OKAY, THIS NEXT PART IS IMPORTANT.

If it were the olden days of my mom and my dad's teenager years, that would mean "going steady." In our world "going out" doesn't mean "go out on a date" it actually means we're bf and gf.

He says "go out" with this super pissed-off quality hanging on to all of it, like ugly brown ornaments of boredom. But that's the way jocks talk, like "Do yuh?" Like, I hafta be asking you this cuz I hafta.

So I just say "Okay," and there you have it, me and Todd are a couple now. He's my actual bf, which is nice, now I have someone. In a way I wasn't allowed to be with anyone else anyway, because he acted quite mightily as if he owned me; like I heard him say once, "Klein is Mine."

So now it's at least official. Everyone always wants to know if we're going out, and now I can say "Yes, we are going out," without worrying how it would get back to him.

Because Alan is sixteen, next thing you know, he drives us all home. We get to the corner of the cul-de-sac where me and Donna live and everyone's like, "Good-bye," so we all make out for a good five minutes. Next we all say actual "good-byes" and us two girls (us) get out of the car. And believe it or not, me and Donna both go into our prospective houses fast as fast can be, which is weird, right, if you think about it? Because wouldn't you just assume the news that I now have a boyfriend would be a big piece of news for a girl to share with her best friend? But instead, I actually space on the entire piece of news. I just go in my house until tomorrow.

Why? Maybe it's because I don't even care that I am now in a full-fledge relationship. Maybe that's because my words are with Todd but my heart, my soul, my mind, and my sex appeal are with Vincent.

So I go into my house and my dad is in front of the TV, nose facing straight up to the ceiling, sound asleep. Giant snore honks coming from him. Gross.

Of course it doesn't even occur to me to wake him up and say I'M HOME, DAD. If he IS waiting up for me, I wouldn't know it cuz he's asleep. And if he's asleep, how would he know if I even got raped or killed? That's the point I always want to make when anyone implies that my dad waits up for me.

Chapter Eleven

When I go upstairs after my date, I go right upstairs. My mom's door is closed so I can't tell her the (pretend) good news (whoopee me and Todd are steady) but instead Maura's door is open. I walk into her room and she's lying wide awake on her bed in the same old sweatshirt. I go, "Hey," and she goes, "Hey," and I go, "What are you listening to?" and she goes, "Hall and Oates," and I go, "Oh."

Then I tell her me and Todd are going out and she's like, "Cool." But I know she's secretly not.

Then I figure I may as well bring up the topic that she knows lies beneath everything else in our household, i.e., her boobs. "So I heard you want surgery," I say, careful not to mention the word boobs.

"So?" she asks, like I'm accusing her of being wildly wrong. And we sit there in silence for a while. Finally she gathers up the courage to explain to me what had been underneath all of this trauma.

"They're gross," she says, "they've gotten way too big. And Julie Kerbin did it anyway."

I'm like, "I don't know Julie Kerbin?"

And she's like, "Well, she looks much better and not like a fat old lady anymore."

And I'm like, "You're not a fat old lady," and she's like, "You're a bold-faced lie" and then she's like, "No guys even like me now. They're all scared that my boobs are too huge." And I'm like, "That's a dumb reason, to change yourself for boys."

And we both hang lightly above the silence of that lie. It is a lie for we all know that, yes of course, we change ourselves for boys.

Duh.

To switch the subject I say, "What about that Filipino guy who plays the tuba that you asked to the Turnabout dance that one time?" And she goes, "I liked him, but then he started liking somebody else and besides his lunch always stinks. He *is* Filipino, you know."

And we laugh so hard until I say good night.

Chapter Twelve

A few days later is Saturday so of course me and Donna are at the mall going to get duck shoes. She's getting chocolate brown; I want bright (kelly) green because Courtney T. has them, but don't tell anyone that's the reason.

While we're there we're trying to decide what to do tonight, so she goes, "Shit on a shingle, there are no parties." And I go, "Plus Todd is in Snowmass with his cousins." And suddenly it occurs to me we should have a sleepover.

Me and Donna.

At her house.

Then it's almost as if someone turned on all the lights at the mall. Everything is bright and happy and the gross booger part of the duck shoes are even beautiful, because now there's a chance I will have Vincent. Even if I will have him for a moment in my mind, don't you see? We will not be alone together but we can be in the same room and I can bathe in the luxurious glow of the way he looks at me, breathing me as if with dragon's breaths. For his eyes will be mine to enjoy, and I will be able to see myself through the way he sees me.

So I say it. "Hey, maybe we could just do nothing and have a sleepover at your house?"

"But won't that be boring beyond?" asks Donna.

"We could watch a Betamax?" I ask her. They have a new Betamax and when they first got it they got like twenty movies as a library.

"That's a great idea!" she says. And would you believe that my heart starts to beat? So, that day in the afternoon we get home from the mall and I go to my mom, "I'm sleeping at Donna's," and she says, "Great, no parties honey?"

And I say, "No parties."

"Do you want Maura to come with you to Donna's house so all three of you can have a sleepover?" she asks me. Then, unfortunately, we all get awash with the sadness of the moment: of course I don't want Maura to come. For we all know that Maura has truly nothing to do on a Saturday night.

But I am polite so I say, "Um, maybe not *this* weekend," and my mom says, "Oh, I just thought I'd check," and we can be certain that my mom and Maura are going to end up watching *Barney Miller* in the living room.

And while my mom and Maura are in the living room, all the while, my dad will be upstairs, flat in his bed, legs out in front of him like matchsticks, reading book after book after book about how people made lampshades out of the skin of Jewish people.

Chapter Thirteen

That night, after forever it seems like, we're actually at Donna's house. Everything is balled up in me. I hear Vincent's footsteps upstairs on the main level. We are in the basement on the coolness of the blackness of their leather couches: she is on one, I am on another, and Vincent must be in the kitchen. I haven't seen him yet, so in my mind, he is wearing his blue bathrobe because I have no clothes with which to dress him in.

We're watching *Godfather*, which is a movie I have always

wanted to see but my parents wouldn't let me. And we're halfway bored, halfway interested, perhaps ambivalent if that's the correct usage of the word. Although I am enjoying looking at the Italian men and imagining every single one of them is a part of Vincent.

Donna's like, "Do you wanna do makeovers?" and I'm like, "Sure," so she runs upstairs and gets a bunch of her mom's makeup and she does me first. We sit in T-shirts Indian style across from each other on the floor.

Out of nowhere Donna says, "I wanna make you look like a prostitute," like she knows what I'm thinking.

(Ha! If she did know, it would be "a prostitute for my dad!" Ha! Ha! Ha!)

But we both giggle at the idea, the simple generalness of the hilarity of the idea of prostitutes, and I go, "Okay."

First she makes my eyes purple all across the lids, shimmering. Coat after coat of mascara, until my lashes are thick; she blots them while they are downcast on a tissue. Next thing she puts on my cheeks is a pink the color of fuchsia, but it's ever-so light. Now it's time for my lips and normally I am a girl who shies away from color on the lip. I like my pinky gloss, but she starts with a dark dark pink, topped off with the pearliest pink gloss that makes it look like I just ate porkchops.

She gets a mirror and we are both so shocked.

I do look more beautiful than prostitutional. If I was a prostitute I would be a young one like *Pretty Baby,* but I am all bright pink and purples and I am telling you I am so in love with myself I can't wait to go upstairs and show him my face, my T-shirt that clings, plus perhaps even a wee wisp of a slip of panties showing beneath my tee.

I am imagining in the lower layers of my mind that I will stand there before him, awash in my pink and purple glory.

But first I go, "Okay, Donna, lemme do you now; I wanna make you a prostitute," and she goes, "I'm too tired," and we get back on our couches and she promptly falls asleep.

And there I am laying there on one couch like a made-up prostitute in a white tee.

I stare up at the ceiling, and as I said, we are directly underneath the kitchen.

I can hear him. Vincent. In the upper part of the house and now I can see what is my green light: Donna's eyes are closed.

She is asleep, deeply dreaming.

Yes.

Now.

And I think, before I go up to show him myself in my colors and eyeliner, what would my excuse be? Why did I go upstairs? BECAUSE I WAS THIRSTY. That's the easiest answer you can think of.

I get out from under the covers, tee and legs only, and slowly take the stairs upstairs. I know that when I see him I will pretend to be surprised.

(Hoping he likes the way my lips are hot pink!)

Upstairs, up the stairs, how scared are you right now? I can hear the fridge closing, I can't wait to see him, I round the corner into the kitchen and—

YOU WILL DIE.

It's Temma. She looks up, ugly eyes ringed with old grayness, like sag, plus ugly lips ringed with those little wrinkles they all get when they smoke.

Damn.

They switched weeks without telling me.

Chapter Fourteen

And ever since that day I haven't even seen him. I heard around their house that Vincent himself was looking for a house in the Las Vegas area and now that Donna is getting older she won't need as much of a father figure. Anyway, it is clear that college life for their daughter is not far off, not far off at all, and I can't believe that Vincent isn't even thinking about me. But whatever.

And everything in my neck of the woods is taken over by this: Maura SCREAMING HER HEAD OFF about her reduction. She wants that boob job so badly you would die if you heard this:

SLAM! She slams her door.

"WHAT IS WRONG WITH YOU?" My mom and dad ask as they eat their shredded wheat, over and over again. "YOU KNOW WHAT IS WRONG WITH ME," is the answer, then finally, I hear my mom and dad:

"Gordon, why don't you give Barry a call." (Barry happens to be this friend of my dad's, whose family we used to go on vacation with. Barry is a plastic surgeon who in the past has done work on people who've been in horrible accidents. But now that plastic surgery is becoming such a thing he is also known as being the one who will do a very natural-looking nose for you.)

So my dad picks up the phone and calls Barry.

197

"Hey, Barry Boy, Gordy here, listen, I'm wondering what it would run me to get my daughter's boobs hacked off?"

Okay, how much am I lying now????! Of course he didn't say that, but here is what I am trying to say: It's almost as if he was saying: "I want you to get in there and chop chop chop because we got too much boob for the house, frankly, Barry."

Did I just gross you beyond right now? But seriously, try to think about the reality of what is happening if you don't mind! Is it possible he could even get a discount on the surgery because they actually play golf together?

Anyways, I assume his conversation was more along the level of, "Barry, it's me, Gordon. Listen, Barry, Maura is interested in a reduction, and I was wondering if you'd consider a consultation?" And so that night I had this dream, so I woke up crying. This is the dream:

Maura and my mom and me are in the waiting room of Barry Shapiro, M.D. My mom reads *Glamour,* Maura reads *Seventeen.* I don't know why I cannot read a magazine, only that there's a feeling that my hands don't work well enough.

The doctor comes out and says, "Maura, you can come in now." Then Maura goes in and my mom waits because she doesn't realize—and no one realizes—that they are at the doctor's office where they are asking a man what he thinks about the size of a girl's breasts and whether they should be gone from the world forever.

So Mom just reads and reads, waiting-room magazine after waiting-room magazine.

This is my dream, as I am telling it to you.

And then I follow down the hallway to see exactly where this so-called doctor is taking Maura. And I find a door halfway open and enter to find Maura sitting in an examining chair. I walk in and I see this so-called doctor weigh each of her breasts in a bowl on a scale, like a kitchen scale. Then he proceeds to right there—right then and there in my dream—cut them off with a knife.

Then Maura walks out and I follow her. And she comes out and says to our mom with a smile, "I'm done." But she isn't wearing a shirt, she is wearing her own skin and there are two big bloody holes where her breasts should be, but she is smiling and my mom is smiling, and my mom says, "HOW WONDERFUL THAT HE WAS ABLE TO DO IT RIGHT THEN AND THERE! Your father will be thrilled!"

Chapter Fifteen

February 14 is Valentine's Day, and at our school we have a dance which is beyond queer personified, but of course me and Todd are going as a couple. So of course me and Donna go to the mall to choose out our dresses.

Have you heard of this thing called Bunny Hutch? It is a label of a clothing line and they have adorable things. We both have our dad's credit cards so I pick out white with this pink ribbon that weaves through the top, and Donna picks out light eggshell blue because light eggshell blue goes with her eyes. We already have our shoes, simple white pumps because simple is best in a situation such as this.

We have our dresses in hanging bags, and did I tell you I am miserable, beyond? That, in fact, I have been depressingly miserable for what seems like weeks at a time? It turns out two things are true: my sister's surgery is scheduled and what can I do to stop it? NOTHING. Because no one believes a word I say because I am fourteen.

And even worse, the next thing, that thing I was afraid of is actually true: Donna said something like "My dad is in 'escro' in Vegas," and I have no idea what "escro" is but it means he's moving.

I'm offering this up to you so you'll begin to understand my mental state, which is a sad one even though we are at the mall. Donna's like, "I need underwear, so let's go to Limited Express." I actually need underwear and so we get all this underwear and go into one dressing room together to try stuff on. Donna puts underwear on, on top of her underwear, like three pairs, then puts her jeans on, on top of her three pairs of Limited Express underwear and I start laughing hysterical beyond and also start to pile on the pairs of underwear and I'd bet you'd be laughing yourself right now if you didn't know the end of the story which is this: when we left we got busted for stealing! Yes! This is true!

As we are walking back out into the mall, out from the store, we think we are out of danger because we go past the sensor things, no problem. But some stupid narc BITCH was watching us and so we were busted royally; then we had to stand in this little room with three black people who were undercovers (WHO EVER EVEN THINKS BLACKS ARE UNDERCOVERS?) and the store manager.

Next thing you know, they've called our moms. Luckily, Temma is off smoking galore with her boyfriend in some apartment, so she asks my mom to pick up both of us. The store releases us both into the custody of my mom. And here's the hilarious part—we both say to both our moms to not tell our dads, and guess what? Neither one of them does. Cuz my dad doesn't care and Donna's dad is out of town.

Anyways, later, we're dying laughing on Donna's bed because the second insane part of the entire experience is—they didn't even take the underwears back! They called our moms and got us in trouble beyond but they forgot to ask for the merchandise! So we're dying laughing and here's the important part of this tale: I am happy. For once in such a long time. Because I am realizing Wow! Look at me, I'm laughing freely, and even though something horrible happened in the store, I am actually happy for the first time in forever since all of my emotions have been circling around this man Vincent, who for all intensive purposes, ignores my very existence on this earth. And I am now having the thought, "Hey, look, self, I can live without him."

And then all of a sudden there he is.

Vincent.

Standing in Donna's doorway to her bedroom.

I want to hurl myself out of myself, my skin is afire, I haven't even ever felt this way.

Seriously, everything in my you-know-down-there-whatever is at once hot and tight and Vincent looks at me and I look at him. And I am so happy he's back and all I want to say is, loudly, "I WILL MOVE TO LAS VEGAS WITH YOU! I HAVE NO IDEA WHAT 'ESCRO' IS BUT IF IT IS SOMETHING YOU NEED TO GET OUT OF I WILL HELP YOU BECAUSE ALL I WANT TO DO IS BE AT YOUR SIDE!"

"So what's this dance you girls are so excited about?" Vincent asks.

"Valentine's Day dance, Dad, duh," Donna says.

"You girls have dates?"

"Of course, Dad, it's this coming weekend, duh," Donna says.

Then Vincent looks at me, eyes like two cats, and I smile, and all I want to know is, does he feel this too? Is he hot and tight in his thing?

Chapter Sixteen

So as you can probably tell, I am dying but I am now finally alive. Like this: alive in a way I had no idea I needed to be.

It's like my life is now worth something because everything can be around whether I see him or not. So even if I'm at school, I know he is at least in town, I have him located in our subdivision, Chantilly, in that house.

I can place him, is what I'm saying. If I know where he is I can make him all tiny, doing dances in my head, going to pour the cup of coffee, what have you.

Yes, he is back, and I know he is back for just a little while, and I am afraid. I am afraid of how I need to have him so badly. I am thinking constantly that if I can do something, just LET HIM DO SOMETHING TO ME, EVEN IF IT IS SIMPLY CUPPING MY FACE IN HIS HAND! Then maybe he will not move away.

And at this point I don't care if Donna hates me forever, or if one day I become Donna's stepmother because I marry him. For he is in my head like racing trains, in circles. I close my eyes and he is there and nothing else will ever matter again until I can find out if he loves me in the same way, with all the hot and heatedness and everything around it.

And suddenly, I realize: TAKE MATTERS INTO MY OWN HANDS. I have to make it happen myself, I just do. So I'm suddenly all about a plan. And I figure out that on the night of the Valentine dance, my dad is going to teach some tooth thing in Fresno, California. And my mom and Maura are going to be in the hospital overnight because that is the day of her surgery, plus one day post-op.

How weird is it to you that lo and behold Maura's surgery is the night of Valentine's Day dance? And that all of a sudden this gets everyone *in* my life *out* of my life except me. Everyone.

And here's how the mysteriousness is shaping up: I know if I am going to pretend to be sick or come down with a flu, I will have to wait until the last minute. I will wait until the last minute of the day of the dance so that Donna has no choice. You see, she absolutely *has* to be all ready in her dress with her date on the way. Otherwise she too would cancel her evening.

So for now I say nothing, absolutely nothing to anyone. This plan is between me and me alone. I lie in wait, in other words.

So, for now, just as simple digressions from our daily routine, to keep us occupied preparing for the dance, me and Donna play with eye shadows: purple, lilac, periwinkle. We narrow our eyes at ourselves in the mirrors of her bathroom, gently brushing on the colors. But all of these colors are a lie between me and Donna. For she knows nothing.

Inside my stomach turns, churns, for it is all working out exactly according to plan. So much so, that I realized you should never ever plan because the best of all possible plans get handed to you on a plan platter.

Temma's out for a week and Vincent is here, here, in town right now.

It is all according to plan I tell you.

Okay, in this moment, this actual afternoon moment, he is not actually at her house in this moment, but at the hardware store getting a new fitting for that thing that opens the garage door. But he is in town. He is located here in my town in Chantilly in my cul-de-sac and I know Temma is long gone and that the DAY AFTER TOMORROW is the day.

My day, I tell you.

Donna will be at the dance and my dad will be at the tooth thing and my mom and my sis will be getting my sis's boobs chopped, and now I just have to figure out a way to get in a fight with stupid-ass Sternberg so I can cancel my V-Day plans.

But how could we fight I need to ask you? We barely even talk. Sure, he'll write me a sentiment on a card if it's my birthday, but the guy never talks to me. So how will I even get mad at him, I ask myself over and over again.

But that is for tomorrow. Today is for pretending to the world like everything is according to plan. And I know that the answer of how to effect a Valentine's Day debacle in the form of a fight will come to me in its own way.

Meanwhile, Mom and Maura pack and I run back and forth from our house to Donna's, checking everything twice. We try on our dresses and we try on our hairdos and I pick up bits and pieces of conversations that confirm the details of my plan. My mom calls over and gets Vincent on the phone:

"Hi Vincent, Eloise Klein. Well, I'm so glad. Oh good. Yes, Donna told you? Yes, just one night in the hospital, just a routine procedure. The girls will be at that dance and of course Jodi is old enough to stay on her own but I'd just be happier if I knew where she was—Yes. Of course. Terrific. Fabulous. 'Bye."

And it's all set, after the dance, Donna and I are to come home and we'll sleep at Donna's, and Vincent will be there. He will be there waiting, wide awake, to make sure we get home safe and sound.

But I will be there too, waiting wide awake with him, for when it all unravels, I will not be going to the dance. Just you wait and see.

Chapter Seventeen

So today is Friday, Valentine's Day, and I awake with a feeling in my heart that it is attached to an airplane loaded only with heartstrings. And the airplane is so high in the sky that it pulls me everywhere. I bound out of bed, like never before. Usually, me getting up involves slowly pulling major eye boogers out of the corner of my eyes, hearing Maura in the shower, the sound of water in a million pins against her soft back. But today I bounce up, like, isn't it wonderful to be alive?

That morning my dad leaves for the airport and wishes Maura luck on her surgery. "You'll be fine," he tells her. "It's routine surgery, they do hundreds of these a day." I swallow my feelings as well as the words I would be saying if I could: That if my sister wants to cut her boobs off then it's her business. And what can I do?

He hugs her and she cries just a little from one eye and I'm thinking, if you're crying now why don't you just cancel? But here's the horrible part: I don't even want her to cancel. Because my plan is in place, so if God came down right now and said, "Hey! Jodi Klein! I will cancel your sister's boobectomy, but you can't have your plan with Vincent tonight," I would be, like, "Hey, chop 'em off."

So I guess I'm as bad as everyone at this point.

I hug Maura and remember the feeling of the very last time I have in my whole lifetime to feel her big squishy boobs through my shirt and I really love them, both of them, but of course, I can't say, " 'Bye boobs, I love you so," so I just say what everyone says: "You're gonna be fine."

She says what everyone says, "Have fun at your dance," still with just one tear in one eye, because wouldn't you imagine at this point she might be scared? I would.

So then I go over to Donna's pretending as though it's a normal day, not the most insanely important day in the world. And I know Vincent is in the house, so when I first get to Donna's, I don't even say "WHERE IS HE?" Instead, I save him like a partially used candy bar for later.

All throughout that Friday at school, I'm not even angry at the world and I convince myself that my sister will be better off without her boobs and maybe even popular. And Spanish is funny and I don't let myself do any imaginings with Vincent in my mind cuz Tonight's the Night. Gonna Be Alright.

And it is just like THAT! YES! For God smiles upon me in the form that he hands me a solution to how I'm going to get out of the dance that night. God hands it to me on a platter in the form of a note passed to me by Dori (a girl who is actually on the sadly fat side. She is actually hugely grossly fat whereas Steff Beltran is not). And speaking of Steff Beltran, this is what it says on the note: "Did you hear Steff Beltran let all the guys from track kiss her boobs?????!!!!!!!!"

And I write back, "Oh my God are you serious????!!!!"

And she writes back "JK."

Which means just kidding.

But here's what I did as my own moment of figuring out how to get my way: I LITERALLY pretended as if I never saw the "JK," I even turned the paper over and over as if she wrote no answer on it at all and shrugged. Doing an act for no audience. My body is doing shrug work for my evil plan, for you see, my body even knows that what is on that paper is golden and important before my brain figures it out. Because now I know exactly what to do.

Sadly, my plan involves spreading Vicious Rumors, which we know is wrong, and cruel. But in this case it is because of a Larger Cause, which, as we have learned in Social Studies, is morally just.

Example: Lying is okay if a Nazi asks you where a Jew is hiding. You can say, "I don't know," and you're not being morally wrong.

So after class I rush to Donna and we walk like two things stuck together down the hall, just one head between us, me saying: "Oh my God, I am so dying right now, you are never going to believe what I just heard about Steff Beltran!"

So I tell her what was on the note, and she's like, "Every guy?"

And I'm like, "They were having a pizza thing after they lost regionals and she came over and one of them made a joke like 'Hey, Steff, donchya know it will cheer me up if you let me kiss your boobs.'"

All of this is coming out of me so fast you would have no idea I was making it up. Like the pizza part? The pizza part is made up by me!

And Donna was like, "Seriously?"

And I was like, "YES! All the guys were like, 'We will all feel better if we all get to kiss your boobs,' and so she let every guy on track team kiss her boobs!"

So Donna's like, "When exactly did this happen?"

And I'm like, "I SAID, Regionals."

And she's like, "Regionals?!"

And I'm like, "Regionals." And we both know what that means if you have half a brain.

Regionals was AFTER Todd asked me to go steady.

So Donna follows me as I huff over to Todd's locker.

"Todd," I go.

"What?" he goes.

I go, "I heard what happened at that thing after you guys lost Regionals. I heard what happened with Steff Beltran."

"Nothing happened with Steff Beltran," he goes.

I go, "Yeah, right. Let it be known that because of your web of lies I'm breaking up with you right now, so you can just forget about the dance tonight."

AND THEN I START TO CRY! I'm serious, I should get an Academy Award or even two at this point because I'm actually crying, just sobbing, and Todd's like, "I didn't do anything!"

But Donna drags me away as though I'm grief stricken

down to the ground. And she goes "Oh my God, he is the worst liar; it's so obvious he lied just then," and I'm like "Yup, yup," sobbing all the while.

Next we go into the girls' bathroom, and the bright light from dusty glass brick windows on high illuminates us so clearly I can see right into the blackheads of Donna's zits. My feelings are a little fluttery at this moment because I know that after my Vincent Plan is complete, I will have to stanch the flow of this rumor (for you and I both know it actually isn't fair). I just have to hope Donna doesn't tell the whole school in less than an hour. Because as much as Steff Beltran is a fat stupid bitch I wouldn't like to see her reputation go down the drain in flames all because of me. And while we are in the white white bathroom I notice that the graffiti on the wall says in the most ironical way, "Stefanie Beltran is whore." So, for now, I am willing to take it as a sign from God that I did the right thing after all.

Donna wipes my eyes with those hard brown paper towels and looks me deep and goes:

"Jodi?"

And I'm like, "Yeah?"

And she's like, "Is it okay with you if me and Marcus still go to the dance?"

I nod.

"But you're going to be all by yourself."

"Oh, I'll be fine," I say.

Chapter Eighteen

"Oh my God, you look beautiful," I say to Donna in her dress. I'm at her house, and we're in her room, and I'm watching her get ready. Boy, does she look good. Her hair looks amazing and her eyeshadow is cornflower, setting off her cornflower eyes. And the doorbell rings and it's Marcus.

I run down and let Marcus in.

Vincent is there.

We almost catch eyes, but no.

He is wearing gray sweatpants as well as brown slippers with sheepskin and an old black polo with red polo player. Me and Vincent welcome Marcus in and we all just stand there in the foyer.

Down the stairs Donna comes like a piece of cake from the camera commercials, blue-trimmed-white in a flirty flow, shoes wobbly à la baby sheep feet.

Click, click, pictures—I take some, Vincent takes some; Donna and Marcus prepare to head out the door.

"Do you have everything?" I ask, like I'm her mom. "Do you have your lip gloss?"

"Yes, I have my lip gloss," she answers me.

Marcus goes ahead of her by a weency bit and as she's on her way to her car and the reality of the moment hits her, she finally turns around and looks at the two of us.

"Wait," she says. She stops, dead in her tracks, then looks at me.

"So. Jodi. You're just gonna sleep at YOUR house then? Instead of here?"

She says this to me.

Time stops, in a way because of my fear, for I had been hoping that she would just leave without leaving behind this question. My eyes watch as the driveways of all the houses move like
lively snakes, around, like cement W's and U's. I make a face,
like Duh? What a question? Also like my mind is on the driveways, playing half interested.

"I'll figure it out," I say, trying to mean everything and nothing in one.

"You just have fun," I say. She waves at both of us and gets in
her side door of the car. Then she buckles in and they drive off.

Chapter Nineteen

Vincent and I are in front of the house. The neighborhood has
never been quieter, seriously. It's six-thirty-ish, just getting dark
and I'm so serious. Nothing has ever been quieter than this moment.

Vincent looks at me.

I go, "Um, I can—" I tilt my head toward my house—

He goes, "I told your mom you were staying here. Did you
call her and tell her you changed your mind about the dance?"

"Nah," I said.

He smiles at me.

I smile at him.

"Where would you like to stay?"

I look at him, begging him to tell me what to do.

But this is all I have, this moment. If I say the TRUTH,
which is MY GOD I'M FOURTEEN OF COURSE I

CAN STAY ALONE IN MY HOUSE, I'M NOT A
DORK!—then I'll have to go to my house. His cat eyes look at
me.

"Where would you feel the most comfortable?" he asks.

"Um, I guess I'll just hang out here if that's cool with you," I
say, and with that he closes the door.

Chapter Twenty

Have I made it sound to you like Chantilly is not beautiful?
Have I made it sound like all the greens are the same? All the
greens are not the same. There is dark forest green, which is the
color of most of the bushes, there is that robin hood green, which
is the color of many shaped trees, then you have the preppy
green of grass.

Chantilly can be beautiful, but if you got the impression that
it is mostly air, you are right.

Me and Vincent move from the foyer into the family room
which happens to be attached to the kitchen. Their family room
couches make an L-shape around the TV, which PS seems to be
standard in nearly every home I visit. Except the Tausigs', who
have theirs in a U-shape due to their many matching leather sec-
tional pieces and enormous TV set.

So Vincent takes his place on the couch. The couch facing the
TV. Not the longways couch where you put your legs along the
length of the couch to watch TV, but rather the couch where you
may wish to put your legs on the coffee table. Don't get mad at
me if I am giving you every single detail. I am simply wanting

you to join me in this moment as best as is uniquely possible.

There are many split-second decisions in his decision to take this position, but I do not yet feel prepared to make my own split-second decision. I say that I am going to the kitchen for something and proceed to find myself a Tupperware thing of chips.

While I am in the kitchen I am telling myself, GO OUT THERE AND SIT RIGHT NEXT TO HIM—GO OUT THERE AND SIT RIGHT NEXT TO HIM—GO OUT THERE AND SIT RIGHT NEXT TO HIM (as opposed to the other couch). And I am saying it like I am a hypnotist and I myself am the patient. I get a paper plate from the paper plate drawer, my hands shaking, and I empty a nicely sized mound of chips onto the plate. Next, I put away the chips and seal up the Tupperware and walk like a two-handed robot with my plate toward the living room where Vincent is sitting bald with the remote pointing straight out.

"Anything you want to watch?" he asks me. And I use the fact that we are amidst the conversation to be blindly blithe about where I sit. And with that, I sit right next to him, plop. There goes the plate of chips, right to the table where it belongs. He moves ever so ever so slightly, perhaps a half an inch, closer to me—and there we are, on one couch together facing the TV.

"Nothing at all?" He asks next, but I don't answer because I am busy listening to the loud parade of oh-my-God-ness in my brain.

"What day is it?" I say calmly, like an adult. Because for real, I have no clue what day it is today. And then I realize it's Friday—*Love Boat* and *Fantasy Island,* which is fine.

He presses his button on the remote like a gun at the TV and it switches to 7. Now we are alone with Channel 7, which has the end of the news and the little commercials that let us know that *Love Boat* will be imminent.

I feel I have to look at him with the side of my face. We are both watching the TV which is to the front of our faces, but he is to one side of me so I have to see him with my cheek. My ear feels his ear, the shape of his face, the black where his sideburn tries to point to his chin.

This moment must have been the moment his face felt my face because this is the moment where he turned to look at me. And smiled.

Like, "Hello, Jodi, here we both are on this couch" smile— with a side order of nervousness. I am feeling an awareness, I might add, about everything, and even the way he is holding his mouth, for sure. A definite slight nervousness, because he can sense, perhaps, much like me, that within his very soul song, this is the night.

My legs are bare on the couch and I am a statue of a posing dove. I am wearing an extra-large pink polo with tiny maroon polo player, stretched out and overwashed. The polo shirt is so long and stretched out so that it covers my jean shorts and my toes play with the hem of it, pulling. In the shape of my pink cotton statuette I feel like one thing. All curled up in my place on the couch.

"So it's too bad you have to miss the dance," he says. "Get in a fight with your boyfriend?"

My God, we, me and him, are suddenly so much more interesting than *Love Boat*. This actual live show, right here, between me and him is the best show I have ever seen in my life.

It is him and me. I want to star in it every second of my life and I want no one to ever come home—no Donna, no mom and no sister, no stupid dad, just me and him.

"Yeah, uh, he's a big dork," I say and move my toes around my hem, changing the shape of my statue. Vincent turns to look at me a hundred percent of the time now. It is almost as if he has been waiting for this moment as madly and as badly as have I.

"So what happened that you had to cancel?" he asks.

"Oh, he, whatever, he lied to me," I say, and then I smile. And now it is so cold that I have to pull my arms in from my statue and hold them inside my pink shirt, pulling my arms in tight underneath my shirt. Folding my arms across myself to cover everything.

"Really," Vincent says.

"Yeah," I say.

"What did he lie about?" Vincent wipes his mustache as if interested in something else, anything other than being directly interested in my story.

"Some whatever girl . . . thing. He didn't exactly lie; he just left something out about something he did with another girl."

There is a pause here when I realize that if I say much more, then me and him will be on a boat to dangerous territory.

And I ask myself, Self, am I ready to set sail in this tiny boat of me and him and boobs being kissed? And before I can even finish this thought his sentence is there:

"So what did he do with another girl?"

"Kissed her—*bluhfruh,* or something like that," is what I say.

"Excuse me?" Vincent asks, polite now, just seemingly interested in the facts of the case, like a police officer.

"He, kissed her—whatevers," I say, then, "I don't need to explain the whole story." Because I'm realizing suddenly that the details of this are too disgusting. And that if I were to tell him the whole story he might actually gross himself out.

So even though I'm shivering in veritable coldness, the room feels so hot now you don't even know. You don't even know how hot it feels that me and this man should be even discussing things about sex, sex appeal, and the like.

Vincent says, "That's okay, Jodi, feel free, tell me what happened." He appears to be concerned and even a little worried in a way a parent might be concerned, with a serious line through the forehead that bespeaks needing to know the details.

"Okay," I say, "there's this girl and I heard there was this rumor going around that she let the track team kiss her boobs-orwhatever right after Regionals because they were all sad about losing."

"She let them do what?"

For God knows what reason I embellish in a way that I cannot seem to stop what is coming out of my mouth. I want him to know everything and nothing at once so I dive in and go for it.

"Okay," I say, "so they were all over at this guy's house and she lives next door so she went over there." I say this because I want to make sure he knows she was asking for it, that if she hadn't gone over there on her own accord, none of this would have happened.

"Because whatever," I add. "Everyone knows she's a slut galore. And they're all hanging around and the captain of track with the entire track team watching says to Steff—"

"Steff who?"

And I say, "Stefanie Beltran," and he says okay.

And I say, "So the captain of track goes, 'We're totally

bummed we lost' or whatever, 'and maybe if I kiss your boobs I will feel better.' "

At this point Vincent is totally enraptured and encapsulated with me. This is the most important story he has ever heard in his life and he is not letting one drip of it get away. He wants to hear the end of the story so I am getting to it as fast as I can.

"Go on," he says.

"So of course these guys are totally joking, it's just a completely hysterical hypothetical to them. But Steff has no idea they're joking so she's like, 'Okay,' and they're like, 'OKAY?' And she's like, 'Okay, you can kiss my boobs.' And they're all like cool! And this is taking place in just the kitchen of the house, the entire track team, Varsity AND frosh-soph! And she takes her shirt off and she's wearing a bra and I guess she's pretty big, or whatever, she's not thin like me and Donna, whatever."

And I realize that I mentioned his daughter but he brushes right past this. This is just me and him.

"She's . . . voluptuous?" he asks, adding the word to the conversation, like it's a word I have never heard before.

"Yes," I say.

And then I go, "And my boyfriend was actually in the room for this event." I nod sadly.

"And this makes you jealous?"

"No!" I say. Why won't he get it? "He didn't just watch. They ALL did it," I say, and we both realize the sadness of the situation.

"But even though it's sad beyond," I say, "she kept going up to each boy, even the boys who had planned in their mind like they were only going to watch this thing and then get the hell out, and kept being like, 'Okay, it's your turn to kiss my boobs,' or whatever."

"I see," says Vincent.

And then I say, "But that is way too gross to even exist and I have to believe they're lying because who would ever want all those guys to be kissing all their boobs in a row?"

So.

FLASH, LIGHTNING.

This is the page you will like to circle because this is where the dirtiest part begins. From saying this next part, this feeling comes over me where lightning splashes down the entire statue of me, like the statue has been electrified by God on high. Vincent looks at me, and it comes out of my mouth because I want the electricity to burn me:

"I mean, maybe it would feel good, who even knows? I haven't ever even done it. But maybe it would feel good," I say.

Vincent looks up at the ceiling like he wants to go somewhere yet his butt is stuck to this couch.

"Do you want to?" I ask him.

"Excuse me?" says Vincent, like he hasn't been hearing any of this right.

"Do you want to show me what it feels like?" I ask him, just like that, like show me how the remote works, show me how it feels to have a boob kissed. And there is the shape of a collapsing cloud blanket between us, and suddenly he is part of my one thing. But instead of a statue of a dove, we are a statue of lovers from the museum.

"Um, I don't think I could do that, honey," he says. "That wouldn't be right," he also says.

"Maybe," I say, "it would only NOT be right if I felt that it was NOT right but if I told you it was FINE then it would be FINE." I am trying to convince him.

He looks at me with this halfway smile, halfway a feeling of hunger and anticipation before a meal that the waitress is about to set on the table. Yet not. Yet a side order of fear alongside it.

He stands up and stretches and makes a noise about what his life is doing to him in this moment.

He walks to the kitchen.

While he is gone I use this opportunity to take my shirt off as fast as fast as I can, and cross my arms around myself. Now I am nothing but tan skin, white bra, short shorts, plus lip gloss.

He comes back in the room and shakes his head like OH NO. I look up at him, afraid of and yet alivened by what he sees.

His eyelashes dance down my chest and skin, and he walks straight toward me. All of the Chantilly greens I mentioned earlier from the neighborhood come flying in through the window. I am fluttered with love everywhere, and if I can take this moment and hold it forever, then hell, I am going to.

See, I don't want the book to end, this is the reason I had to write this down to tell you, this feeling right here. And if I can stay here together in his eyes touching me forever, I could stop living because I would be dead but fine.

He walks over to the couch and kneels down before me to my level. Are you dying right now? He takes my little white bra strap on just one side of me and lowers it, lowers it, ever so slightly in a slow way, to my shoulder and then he does the same with the other one.

Now two straps are down and I am sitting there à la a

Princess in a Strapless Disney Dress, shoulders totally exposed, heart-shaped across my breasts like the top of the dress I would be wearing if I were at the dance tonight.

So I am sitting here with my bra straps down and he scoops out one breast with his big hand, and puts it atop the bra part, then scoops out the other breast and sets it the same way, and now I am the most beautiful light-infused thing in the world. My whole torso is alive with magnetism and it all resides in a tightness that is clumped up in a hot way I have never felt before, never, I tell you.

He lowers his bald brown Italian head, his long black lashes downcast and sensuous, and kisses one breast. His lips land atop the white not-tanned part of one and leave a wet part, then he sends his lips over to my other and kisses the skin on it like that.

Then all of a sudden, he is not kissing anymore, he is licking one and holding the other, and then he starts doing what seems like Frenching my breasts. Now I feel like I might want to throw up because he makes out with them so much, they're like old familiar friends that he loves and misses; he even seems like he cries on them.

And me? I disappear into the ceiling and fly around, far and above Chantilly, no more legs to walk on, just flying around, my back arched over everyone's house, cars parked, garages closed for the night, most of the people are tucked in and they have no idea I fly. I fly around in fast circles as I let him kiss and touch and hold and suck whatever he can get in his mouth for as long as he possibly can and I am all flowers alive across the sky. With my body arched, I leave Chantilly and fly over the city where there are bridges and lights, cloudily climbing into the nether regions of the clouds so I can fly high in the sky to Paris or France, or anywhere around the world. It can be Ghana, Africa, or deepest jungles, flying swirling spirals around highest of sky until I land in cloudlike high

Ahhhhhhhh

I am so far I am upside down in the sky now, and then, RII-IIIIIIIIIIIIIIING.

The phone rings.

Just like that and we both jump so fast you would of thought that we were both cats jumping out of our skin. Who could it be? No one knows, and I pull my big polo shirt down so fast over my wet breasts, that I don't even put the bra parts back on over—and his pants are straining and he has the largest boner of all time immemorial, and it pokes at his pants making it difficult for him to move toward the telephone at all.

He grabs for the telephone; he stops to catch his breath for a mere moment. For he must not communicate even a moment of this moment to anyone on the other line, I suppose.

"Huh-lo?" he says.

And I can hear my mom's voice, so tiny and Jewish in the distance:

"Vincent? Eloise Klein here. When Jodi gets back from the dance can you please let her know that her sister's surgery went well? And that her sister is resting comfortably?"

"Yes, I'll do that," Vincent says, not bothering to let my mom know I blew off the dance and was sitting here on the couch having just having gotten my tits licked.

Chapter Twenty-one

That moment was the end of that moment for a million reasons, mostly allowing to the fact that we came to our senses.

He looked at me after this point where he's hung up the phone and he's standing and his penis is so hard and literally pointing at me through the gray sweatpants that it is beyond funny. I have never seen anything like it and it's literally bigger than like two to three of Todd Sternberg's from that day from the pool and I believe Vincent was frightened.

I AM NOT KIDDING YOU! He looked at his dick like it was a size of which he'd never been before, and I must of had the greatest look of sheer terror. And with that, he went running up the stairs as if he had to go poo like crazy.

While he was out of the room I put each of my two wet breasts back into their bra compartments and stood up and stared at the plate of chips on the coffee table.

Hello, chips, I think to myself. Did you see that?

And then I could have sworn I heard him upstairs, sounding as though he were angry at his very own penis, as if he was looking though the bathroom cabinets to find something with which to cut it off! And I stand up and head through the foyer, yelling at the top of my lungs, "ACTUALLY YOU KNOW WHAT? I CAN STAY ALONE AT MY HOUSE TONIGHT, I'M PRACTICALLY FIFTEEN."

And he calls back something muffled like, "MURFLAGE-DRUEM."

And I run out, and run over to my house.

Chapter Twenty-two

First thing I do is run upstairs to my room and lay down.

Think for a minute.

Then run down the stairs back to the living room for the bolster from the couch which is my favorite and then run back upstairs to my room and hold it tightly between my legs like the biggest softest rocket you ever saw and rub and rub and rub, all the while an image of Vincent I've placed at the door, watching.

Chapter Twenty-three

If you are wondering what I look like, maybe it's because you haven't completed the picture of me yet and you've only imagined my whole book with an empty cloud at the center of it.

But after I finished laying on my bed with my big soft rocket between my legs, I felt better so I went and looked in the mirror. I will share with you what I saw so you can see too.

This is me, Jodi K:

I tilt my head to the side when I look at myself in the mirror. I have brown hair and brown eyes like your average Jewish person, although I think my eyes might be sad in the pretty way, like I need you to hold me. I am tan and I am skinny and I look good with white-colored clothes, bra, etc., against my skin.

I guess I look like a woman viz-a-viz my body nowadays. I mean, I do look like a woman. Not I guess. I know what I look like and by the way, I am certain that it's sexy.

Epilogue

A few weeks after that, Vincent moved to outside of Las Vegas, Nevada, taking a part of my sexiness with him. By this time I had fallen deeply in love with him and had started to spend every second of every day scheming as to how to make us alone together again. But everytime he saw me, he looked at me with complete terror, very much the way I looked at his actual penis in the sweatpants shape when it appeared to be giant.

Every so often he would see me with Donna, coming home from the spring days of school, in flip-flops, and then he would walk in the opposite direction, or his car would tear out of the driveway. And before you knew it he was out of "escro" and a free man living in Vegas.

After that for a little while Donna would go on a weekend trip to see him in Vegas and I knew full and well I couldn't go with her. So I didn't even ask.

Epilogue Part Two

Me and Todd Sternberg got back together after I let it be known that believe it or not nothing ever happened with the track team and that it was nothing more than a vicious rumor.

Can you believe it?

Todd is my boyfriend now, because it would only be in another world I could have Vincent as my man, my one true man. I am in high school and Todd is in high school and we actually look quite cute together. He has his own ways to find my sexiness, and they are nothing like me and Vincent.

Vincent discovered me and opened me up, like a present. Todd and me play together like secret backyard animals, like teammates of what do we know, what don't we know, and how do we find it together. On a scavenger hunt for what is sexy.

And I am happy to tell you that since me and Todd moved through the world together in many ways, now I even find he is starting to open up his heart to me a little bit. Seriously, he has added to his vocabulary a few more words than "Yuh" and "Nah" and "Whatever" and one week ago on my birthday card he signed it, "I LOVE YA!!!!!" Which was so sweet, I am starting to think I might actually love him too.

Steff dropped out of school because of the rumor. How sad that she would let people's opinions of her form so much of her self-esteem. Yet in a way it was another true case of moral aptitude because one person was sacrificed for the greater good. Steff had to leave but I got to be with Vincent.

Vincent, who became nothing but a man running from my eyes, was a fleeting, disintegrating starlite for me. Each time he came back to Chantilly, he would put a box or a trunk in his car, take a little more with him, until there was nothing left.

One More Epilogue

I got my period and I turned fifteen.

Last Epilogue Ever I Promise

I never even told you my sister came back from her surgery the day after the Valentine's Day dance, and me and Victor's triumphant yet sadly too-real moment of connectivity. And she was fine.

She cried a little to a lot in her bedroom, and kept wanting to borrow old polos of mine that were even too small on me because they put pressure on her bandages and that made them feel better. She would wear my tight old T-shirts to hold her bandages in close and closer, then one actual bigger T-shirt over it to hide the big stack of scars that was her chest.

My dad came back from his conference, and seemed the same except there was a moment where he took one look at Maura's new improved body and the flatness in her shirt and I could swear his vomit almost came up his throat, caught in him, as if to choke.

And he was definitely changed that day. I don't know what caught hold of him. Something small, like a little imperceptibleness of change, with the only addition that he completely stopped reading his Holocaust books.

ABOUT THE AUTHORS

ERIC ALBERT's e-mail address is Eric.Albert@alumni.brown. edu. He welcomes all correspondence.

GRETA CHRISTINA is the editor of *Paying for It: A Guide by Sex Workers for Their Customers* (Greenery Press). Her writing has appeared in both *Ms.* and *Penthouse* magazines, *Best American Erotica,* and several other anthologies. You may contact her and read more of her writing at www.gretachristina.com.

JILL SOLOWAY is a television writer most of the time, but also likes to write fiction. She is the award-winning writer/producer of *Six Feet Under;* has written the film adaptation of David Sedaris's *Me Talk Pretty One Day,* and is the cocreator of the acclaimed literary/performance showcase *Sit 'n Spin.* Her new book, *Tiny Ladies in Shiny Pants* (Free Press), is coming out in fall 2005.

ABOUT THE EDITOR

SUSIE BRIGHT is the editor of the bestselling *Best American Erotica* series and is founder of the *Herotica* series, as well as the author of some of the most influential books in contemporary sexual politics, including *Mommy's Little Girl: Susie Bright on Sex, Motherhood, Porn, and Cherry Pie.* She hosts the weekly audio show *In Bed with Susie Bright,* on Audible.com, and she performs and teaches creative writing and sex education throughout the world. She lives in northern California with her partner and daughter, and can be found at www.susiebright.com.

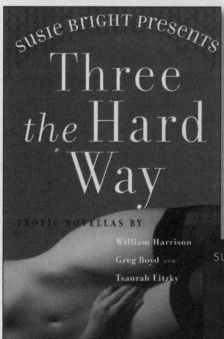